SPECIAL MESSAGE TO READERS

This book is published under the auspices of

THE ULVERSCROFT FOUNDATION

(registered charity No. 264873 UK)

Established in 1972 to provide funds for research, diagnosis and treatment of eye diseases. Examples of contributions made are: —

A Children's Assessment Unit at Moorfield's Hospital, London.

•

Twin operating theatres at the Western Ophthalmic Hospital, London.

•

A Chair of Ophthalmology at the Royal Australian College of Ophthalmologists.

•

The Ulverscroft Children's Eye Unit at the Great Ormond Street Hospital For Sick Children, London.

You can help further the work of the Foundation by making a donation or leaving a legacy. Every contribution, no matter how small, is received with gratitude. Please write for details to:

THE ULVERSCROFT FOUNDATION,
The Green, Bradgate Road, Anstey,
Leicester LE7 7FU, England.
Telephone: (0116) 236 4325

In Australia write to:
THE ULVERSCROFT FOUNDATION,
c/o The Royal Australian and New Zealand College of Ophthalmologists,
94-98 Chalmers Street, Surry Hills,
N.S.W. 2010, Australia

HOMESTEADERS' WAR

When Wilbur Daniels and his fellow homesteaders are faced with tax demands from the Crossville council, they are up in arms. However, they find support from the ex-sheriff, Luke Tilling, a drunkard who is suffering from a personal tragedy. As bullets begin to fly, a powerful landowner seizes his chance of getting rid of the homesteaders. Not even the beautiful Cordelia can prevent Luke from taking his life in his hands. Will he survive, or will tragedy strike again?

Books by Tom Parry
in the Linford Western Library:

THE BANDIT TRAIL
LAST STAGE TO SULA
RICCO, SON OF RINGO
SHOWDOWN AT TOPEZ
FERNANDO'S GOLD
MEXICAN SHOOT-OUT

TOM PARRY

HOMESTEADERS' WAR

Complete and Unabridged

LINFORD
Leicester

First published in Great Britain in 2006 by
Robert Hale Limited
London

First Linford Edition
published 2008
by arrangement with
Robert Hale Limited
London

British Library CIP Data

Parry, Tom, *1930 –*
Homesteaders' war.—Large print ed.—
Linford western library
1. Western stories
2. Large type books
I. Title
823.9′14 [F]

ISBN 978–1–84782–130–0

Published by
F. A. Thorpe (Publishing)
Anstey, Leicestershire

Set by Words & Graphics Ltd.
Anstey, Leicestershire
Printed and bound in Great Britain by
T. J. International Ltd., Padstow, Cornwall

This book is printed on acid-free paper

1

The homesteaders had called an urgent meeting. Of the twenty families involved only seven men attended.

'Is this all who are going to come?' demanded Wilbur. He was the eldest of the group, a whiskered Texan who had been in the cavalry when they fought the Indians. After the Indian wars he had accepted the forty acres of land which the government had allotted those who had applied for it.

At first everything had appeared promising. The work had been hard in clearing the site but he was never one to shirk hard work. The others who had accepted the government's offer had also been a hard-working, friendly lot. They had all got on well together. They were all willing to help each other. If someone was in difficulties, either with his crops or even financially, then the others would rally round. Yes, for the first few years everything had been fine. They had been lucky, too, with the harvests, which had meant that they could cut their corn and store enough in the winter to last them until the following summer. But now suddenly it had all changed.

Bradley had appeared on the scene.

His first appearance had been an inauspicious one. He had turned up at Wilbur's farm a few days before. He was wearing a blue suit and black shoes. He was every inch an office clerk.

Wilbur watched him approach. At the corner of the farm was the slurry which covered a couple of hundred square feet. The slurry was coloured brown and blended with the colour of the earth. If an unsuspecting person approached the farm from the direction in which Bradley was approaching, it was difficult for the untrained eye to see where the slurry stopped and the earth began. Bradley had an untrained eye.

He walked straight into it.

The result was that when he had taken two paces he found that he was up to his ankles in the slurry.

Wilbur was watching him from the porch.

'You'll have to go round,' he called out.

Bradley gingerly extricated himself from the cloying mass which stuck like glue to his shoes. He tiptoed like a ballet-dancer round the slurry. However, when he thought he had reached the edge and could tread on the earth, he was again mistaken. His foot sank into the mess, although this time not quite as far as the bottom of his trousers.

'I'm in a mess,' he said when he eventually reached the front porch.

'Yes, you are,' agreed Wilbur, trying to conceal a smile.

There was a fire in the kitchen and after Bradley had taken off his shoes and tried to wipe as much of the muck off as he could with the duster that

Wilbur had provided, he placed the shoes gingerly in front of the fire.

'They'll dry out there,' he stated.

Wilbur made coffee. Bradley accepted the cup gratefully.

'I'm not really used to travelling around the farms,' he explained.

'So I see,' said Wilbur, drily.

'By the way, I haven't introduced myself. My name is Edward Bradley. Ted to my friends.'

'My name is Wilbur Daniels.'

'I know. I've got it on my list.'

He produced a handwritten list of names.

Wilbur was burning with curiosity to know why Bradley had a list of the names of the homesteaders. However he managed to refrain from asking the purpose of Bradley's visit.

'I'm here on official government business.' Bradley chose that moment to have a drink of his coffee. Wilbur was forced to wait a few moments longer before finding out what that business was.

'You've been on the farm — let me see' — Bradley again consulted his list — 'for seven years.'

'That's right,' said Wilbur, shortly.

'During that time you haven't paid anything towards the town's taxes.'

'So?'

'Well I'm here to see that from now on you and the other farmers will start paying.'

Wilbur burst into laughter.

'Are you kidding, mister? Why should we pay towards the town's lighting? We haven't got any lighting here. We still use oil-lamps and candles. Why should we pay towards the town's water supply? We get our water from the well and our cattle get their water from the river. And why should we pay towards the grand town hall which is being built? None of us farmers will ever use the place. If you think we're going to pay tax you're barking up the wrong tree.'

Bradley again consulted his list. 'It will be forty dollars a year. One dollar for every acre you own.'

'You'll collect it over my dead body.' Wilbur was beginning to lose his temper.

'And since you've been here for seven years you owe two hundred and eighty dollars in back payment.'

'What!'

Wilbur's nearest neighbour, Tom Mullings swore afterwards that he heard Wilbur's cry even though he lived a quarter of a mile away. However because of the lie of the land he couldn't see Wilbur's other reaction to Bradley's statement. It was to seize his visitor's shoes, go to the front door and throw them as far away as he could.

'There, you can fetch those. And tell your bosses that the next time you call, it won't only be the shoes I'll be throwing. You'll be inside them.'

2

At about the same time that Wilbur was throwing Bradley out of his house, Luke Tilling was being thrown out of the Red Garter. That establishment was a saloon in Crossville. If anyone had bothered to count the number of times that Luke had been thrown out of the saloons in Crossville during the past year or so they would have reached two dozen without any difficulty. In each case Luke had become drunk, and being drunk had become belligerent. He usually picked a quarrel with one of the inhabitants in the saloon in which he had found himself. He had challenged the person — who was generally minding his own business — to either a fist-fight or a gunfight. The result was always the same. The owner of the saloon intervened. He called to a member of his staff whose specific duty was to evict troublemakers — and Luke would be thrown out.

Luke picked himself up from the sidewalk. On this particular occasion the assistant in the saloon who had thrown him out had been a big man — well over fifteen stone. Luke's eviction therefore hadn't been a gentle push out through the saloon's double doors. Instead it had been a bodily throw which resulted in Luke landing rather heavily on his side. The sudden painful contact with the sidewalk helped to restore him to sobriety. He staggered to his feet.

Several passers-by had been forced to step off the sidewalk to avoid colliding with Luke. One of them stopped and enquired:

'Are you all right, Luke?'

Her name was Cordelia Dance. She was a pretty young woman who, having passed her twenty-first birthday and having no obvious beaux was often the subject of conversation among the married women in the town. True, her father was the preacher, and some of the wives speculated that being involved with the running of the church as she was, it left little time for any of the normal female activities which involved falling in love and getting married. In fact many of these wives who discussed Cordelia from time to time envied her freedom and independence.

'Yes, thank you, Cordelia.'

Luke tried ineffectively to brush some of the dust from his jacket.

'Just look at you. You're getting thrown out of saloons regularly. Where are you going to end up, Luke?'

'The same place as the rest of the inhabitants of the town. Boot Hill.'

'That isn't what I mean, and you know it,' she retorted angrily.

'I appreciate you being concerned about me, Cordelia, but I can manage on my own.'

He began to weave an unsteady trail along the sidewalk. She caught up with him.

'It doesn't look as though you can

even cross the road on your own.' She took hold of his arm. 'Come on, I'll buy you a coffee. It should help to sober you up.'

He allowed himself to be led into the nearby coffee-house. Cordelia ordered two coffees and they sat at a corner table. Luke stared out through the window while they waited for the coffees to arrive.

'Why, Luke?' she demanded.

'Because it helps me to forget.'

'But it wasn't your fault. And anyway it happened over a year ago.'

'She was a beautiful child. Everybody said that she was a beautiful child.' He was trying in vain to keep the emotion out of his voice.

Cordelia put her hand on his. Their coffees arrived.

'You don't blame the rider from the Box O ranch who ran her down?'

'No. It was my fault. I should have kept hold of Annabelle's hand, then she wouldn't have run out into the middle of the road to fetch her bonnet.'

He was obviously struggling with his memories.

'Why don't you come to church, Luke? Prayer isn't the answer to everything but it can help.'

'Ruth obviously thought it was my fault. She left me straight after the funeral.'

'Ruth was a coward. She should have stayed with you and helped you to fight this feeling of guilt that you've got.'

'Yes, Ruth was weak. But it doesn't stop it all being my fault. I still see her regularly.'

'Who, Ruth?'

'No,' he replied, impatiently. 'Annabelle. I can see her dashing out into the road and the horse knocking her over. I knew straight away that she was dead.'

He stood up. 'Thanks for the coffee,' he said.

As he walked towards the door he didn't see Cordelia wiping the tear from her eye.

3

The first meeting of the homesteaders having come to an abrupt end, due to the lack of support, Wilbur called to see his neighbour Tom Mullings one evening.

'What's going on, Tom?' he demanded.

Tom, having first handed Wilbur a glass of whiskey, replied, 'Most of the farmers haven't the stomach for a fight.'

'We're not talking about a fight. We're talking about our rights as citizens. We've helped the town to grow during these past years. We've sold our surplus grain and livestock in the market. Without our corn to make their bread many of the townsfolk would have had to buy their corn to make their bread from one of the neighbouring towns at twice the price we charge for it.'

'I agree. But the town is growing.

Bradley, when he called here, said that they wanted money for some of the council schemes like new drains, a new road and council offices.'

'Ah, you've hit the nail on the head,' stated Wilbur, eagerly. 'They want us to help to pay for their easy way of life. We'll be helping them to sit in an office all day and push pieces of paper around. Well, I'm not prepared to give in to them.'

'Neither am I,' said Tom, pouring his visitor another glass of whiskey. 'But we've got to tread carefully, Wilbur.'

'What do you mean, Tom?' demanded a puzzled Wilbur.

'You saw how few were at the meeting. I've been asking around. Some of the others have already agreed to pay.'

'The traitors.' Wilbur slammed his fist into the palm of his hand as a sign of his frustration.

'It's their choice,' said Tom, with resignation.

'Hang on a minute,' said Wilbur. 'Do

you mean to say that these farmers are paying the forty dollars and the two hundred and eighty dollars that Bradley is asking?'

'That's right.'

'But how can they afford to pay it? I'd be pushed to find forty dollars without selling some of my stock. And there's no way I could find the two hundred and eighty dollars.'

'It seems they're getting the money.'

'From a bank?'

'No, from Oliver.'

'Not the Box O owner?'

'The same.'

'But why should Oliver lend them money?'

'He's willing to buy some of their stock from them. He'll buy enough to pay for the town taxes and the back payments.'

'But they'll be selling their cows and pigs that they'll need to live on. Especially during the winter.'

'They say that they can manage on less stock.'

'Yes, they say they can manage but wait until we have a hard winter,' said Wilbur, grimly. 'I wouldn't even sell a chicken to Oliver.'

'Neither would I.'

'How many farmers have agreed to this already?'

'About six from what I can gather.'

'We've got to fight Oliver,' said Wilbur, angrily.

'You mean with guns?' said a startled Tom.

'No. Legally.'

'How can we do that? We don't know anything about the law.'

'No. But I've got a nephew in Chicago. He's a lawyer. I'll send him a telegram. I'm sure he'll come to help us out.'

'I don't see how we can get out of paying taxes from now on.' There was more than a hint of resignation in Tom's tones. 'They've got a good argument when they say that most of us farmers send our children to school. We should be helping to pay towards the teacher's wages.'

'All right. I'll go along with that. But there's no way on earth that I'm going to pay the tax for the years gone by.'

'So you think your nephew might be able to help us?'

'I'm sure he will. He's always said he'd like to visit the town. I think he's got some fool notion that it's some kind of marvellous place to live.' He snorted with laughter.

'Maybe it is compared to Chicago.'

Wilbur's refusal of the offer of another drink of whiskey showed how eager he was to get the telegram off to his nephew.

4

The stage was due to arrive in Crossville in about an hour's time. The people inside were all eagerly looking forward to the arrival. This was their third day on the stage and all they wished for was the end of their journey so that they could have a decent meal and a bath.

The journey had been uneventful. Those in the stagecoach comprised two couples and the single travellers, who had become quite friendly largely due to their close proximity for the past three days.

'I used to read about the stagecoach travellers in England in the books by Fielding and Sterne,' said Daisy Crane. 'But I never realized how uncomfortable it could be until I came on this journey. I think I'll have to soak in a bath for a week to get the stiffness out of my bones.' She was the youngest of the travellers and was coming to Crossville to take up a position as a teacher.

'I'll just be glad to get my corset off,' said one of the other ladies on the stage, Mrs Stevens, to general laughter. 'Of course it's all right for you, young lady, since you don't wear one.'

Her husband, who was seated next to her said: 'I can't wait to have a few pints of beer. My throat has never been so dry.'

The person sitting opposite them, who was wearing a clergyman's collar frowned at the suggestion of drinking beer.

'I'll be glad to get to Crossville so that I can prepare for my first service on Sunday.'

The other couple, who had rarely joined in the conversation now voiced an opinion, possibly because of their proximity to their journey's end.

'We can't wait to open our shop,' said the woman, who was in her thirties.

‘What will you be selling?’ demanded Mrs Stevens.

‘Cakes. We’ve bought a shop which we’ll turn into a cake shop.’

‘You’ll all be welcome,’ said her husband, Mr Gibbons, with an embarrassed laugh.

‘I’ll be one of your first customers,’ promised Mrs Stevens.

‘Once she’s inside a cake shop I have difficulty in getting her out,’ said her husband, to general laughter.

‘What about you, young man?’ demanded Mrs Steven of the remaining single traveller. Now that the ice had been broken she felt free to ask the question which she would never have asked at the beginning of their journey.

‘Oh, I’m a lawyer. I’m coming to visit my uncle who wants some legal advice.’

Their conversation was terminated by an unusual sound. It was the unmistakable sound of a shot.

‘That was a shot,’ stated a startled Mr Stevens.

‘It was a long way away, dear,’ said his wife.

‘Maybe it was somebody shooting rabbits,’ suggested Mr Gibbons.

They had all turned their attention to the windows on either side but all they could see was the prairie.

‘The driver is going faster,’ observed the clergyman. ‘Perhaps the shot was intended for us.’

It was indeed obvious that the coach was going faster. In fact it was swaying alarmingly from side to side.

‘Do you think we’re being attacked by outlaws?’ suggested the teacher.

Although the same thought had occurred to all of them, they were quick to dissociate themselves from her suggestion.

‘They don’t have outlaws in these parts,’ said Mr Gibbons, sounding more positive than he felt.

‘At least we know there aren’t any Indians,’ said the lawyer. ‘My uncle fought in the last Indian wars. And they were over almost twenty years ago.’

There was the sound of another shot. This one was unmistakably closer.

'They should have put a shotgun rider on the stage,' said Mr Stevens. 'I think the company was very lax in that respect.'

The next moment the stage came to an abrupt halt. It was so abrupt that the passengers on one side were shot across to the other side. Daisy ended up on the lawyer's lap.

'I'm sorry,' she said with embarrassment, as she regained her seat.

'Everybody out of the coach.'

It was obvious to everyone that the command didn't come from the driver. This was a stranger's voice.

They all trooped out, not knowing what to expect.

They saw six masked men on horseback. All were holding revolvers.

The leader of the outlaws tossed a saddle-bag on to the ground.

'I'm making a collection,' he said. 'I want the men to empty their wallets in the bag and any money that the ladies have in their handbags is to be put in there' He pointed to the lawyer. 'You can make the collection.'

'You'd better do as he says,' called out the driver.

There was a distinct air of reluctance from the travellers to part with their money, but none of them openly refused.

As each one emptied his or her wallets or handbags the outlaw motioned that they could get back into the coach. When it came to the turn of the teacher, she said:

'You should have said: Your money or your life.'

'Get in the coach,' said the outlaw, waving his gun threateningly.

The only one left was the lawyer. He emptied his wallet into the saddle-bag.

'Hand it up to me,' said the outlaw.

The lawyer complied. As he was about to receive it the outlaw, instead of taking hold of the bag, shot the lawyer between the eyes.

5

The funeral of the lawyer, Nigel Wade, was held in Crossville several days later. Considering that he had never lived in the town the turn-out far exceeded the preacher's expectations.

'I've never seen the church so full,' said the Reverend Dance.

'Perhaps we should have a funeral more often,' suggested Cordelia.

Her father frowned at her flippancy.

'Death is a hallowed state,' announced Padlow Gunthorpe, the third person who was in the vestry where they could see through the window the growing congregation.

Cordelia was on the point of making another frivolous remark, but she bit her lip.

'I'll take the main service,' said her father. 'But since you actually met the unfortunate young man, maybe you'll also say a few words.'

'As you wish,' said Padlow, although he was secretly pleased to be able to have the chance to appear in the church pulpit for the first time.

Cordelia, who was still watching the arrivals through the window saw a familiar face.

'I never thought I'd see Luke come to church,' she exclaimed.

'Who's Luke?' demanded Padlow.

'Luke Tilling,' explained Cordelia. 'He used to be the town marshal.'

'But now he's the town drunk,' said the preacher.

'He was struck by a cruel tragedy,' stated his daughter.

'What happened?' demanded Padlow.

'He was walking down Main Street with his young daughter,' explained Cordelia. 'She was holding his hand. Suddenly he spotted a wanted outlaw ahead of him. He let go his daughter's hand for a second in order to draw his gun. During that time his daughter's bonnet had blown off. She rushed across the street to retrieve it. Some cowboys were racing through the street and one of their horses hit the young girl. She died instantly.'

Even in reciting the well-known events Cordelia couldn't keep the distress from her voice.

'Often out of adversity comes happiness,' said her father.

'I wish I believed that,' replied his daughter.

'If it is God's will then we must accept it,' said Padlow, piously.

'I suppose it was God's will that Nigel Wade should have been shot,' snapped Cordelia.

Her father, sensing an argument, diplomatically announced that it was time for them to go into the church.

During the service Cordelia found herself glancing around the congregation searching for Luke. She eventually found him seated in the back row. It gave her a glow of satisfaction to have eventually spotted him.

Her father gave a brief address

emphasizing how the abrupt demise of Nigel Wade was a loss to the community and principally to his family. His uncle, Wilbur was heard to choke back a sob at the mention of the family.

When it came to Padlow's turn to speak, he entered the pulpit with dramatic slowness. He then surveyed the congregation. In fact this gave the congregation a chance to study him. Most of them had heard that since the town was expanding, it had become necessary to take on a curate. So they were studying him with interest.

They saw a young man with a thin, pale face. He wasn't particularly handsome, but on the other hand he wasn't ugly either. Some of the women with single daughters of a marriageable age regarded him with particular interest as a possible future son-in-law. The only obvious drawback about him was that he had rather a high-pitched voice.

His invitation to 'say a few words' by the preacher soon extended to five minutes, then ten, then even longer.

Cordelia glanced at her father who glanced diplomatically towards the church ceiling. The curate gave the deceased several virtues which only a person who had known Wade for a considerable time would have been able to vouchsafe. He made a great deal of the fact that the deceased had been coming to Crossville to help an elderly relative. Padlow presented Wade as a latter-day Good Samaritan. There was a choked sob from Wilbur.

He finally finished glorifying Wade's life. Most of the congregation breathed a sigh of relief. The preacher took over and announced that they would sing the hymn: 'We'll all gather at the river.'

The congregation sang it with gusto — they were glad to release the tension which had built up during Padlow's speech.

After the service the preacher, Padlow and Cordelia stood by the church door as the congregation came out. The preacher shook hands with many of them and introduced Padlow as he did so. Cordelia, who was standing to one side, acknowledged many of the ladies as they left. She was looking for one particular face and she was not disappointed when Luke emerged and, seeing her, approached.

'It's nice to see you, Luke,' she said, with a smile, as they shook hands.

Luke's reply took her by surprise.

'When the dust has settled, I want you to come with me.'

6

In fact it was a couple of days later when Luke made the first of his visits — this was to Wilbur's farm. He skirted the slurry. As Wilbur watched him approach he couldn't but remember Bradley's approach — could it only be less than a fortnight before?

Wilbur shook Luke warmly by the hand.

'Come in, Luke, it's always a pleasure to see you.'

Wilbur knew all about Luke's excessive drinking after his daughter's death and studied him surreptitiously to see whether he was in fact sober.

Luke supplied the answer.

'It's all right, Wilbur, I'm quite sober. In fact I haven't had a drink for the past few days. So before you offer me a drink I'll have to refuse.'

Wilbur smiled.

'It's good news about you not drinking. Although if you change your mind and want a whiskey just let me know.'

'Thanks. But no thanks. I know this will be a painful subject but I've really come to ask you a few questions about your nephew — the one who was shot by the outlaws.'

'I'll tell you all you want to know, Luke. Although I'm puzzled about your interest in the case. You gave up the marshal's position some time back.'

'I know. One of the reasons why I'm asking questions is because I haven't got much faith in my replacement.'

'To be honest, Luke, neither have I. Summers came here yesterday and told me he was doing everything he could to find the outlaws. But he was afraid that they would be a hundred miles away and so there was very little chance of catching them.'

'Why did Summers say the outlaw killed Wade?' asked Luke.

'He said the outlaw probably thought

my nephew was going for his gun when he handed the saddle-bag up to him.'

'I've been talking to the driver of the stage. He saw the whole thing. He said that Wade was holding the saddle-bag in his hand. He was about to hand it to the outlaw. There was no way that your nephew could go for his gun since he was already holding the saddle-bag when the outlaw shot him. His hand wasn't free — unless he was left-handed.'

'He was right-handed,' said Wilbur, shortly.

Luke stood up.

'Thanks, Wilbur. You've told me more or less what I expected.'

'You haven't told me why you're taking an interest in the case,' asked Wilbur, keenly.

'For the moment that's my secret,' replied Luke.

* * *

The following day Cordelia entered the coffee shop and found Luke seated at one of the window-seats. Her face showed her surprise which quickly changed to a smile of pleasure.

'I don't often see you here, Luke,' she observed.

'I've changed my drinking haunt,' he replied, as he ordered coffees from the waitress.

'I hope it's permanent.'

'We'll see,' he replied, enigmatically.

'Is this something to do with the conversation we had after Nigel Wade's funeral?'

'Not entirely. I don't get many chances now to talk to an attractive young lady. I've got to seize the chance while I can.'

She smiled. 'I forgot that you can be quite a charmer when you put your mind to it.'

They stared at each for a few moments.

'Yes, it's one of the things I've been missing,' he said, quietly.

She put her hand over his.

'You know I'll always be here if you want me.'

'As one of your lost causes?'

She snatched her hand away.

'How dare you,' she hissed. The remark was loud enough for the couple at the next table to hear it. They listened avidly for any further snippets of conversation, but both Luke and Cordelia drank their coffees in silence.

When they had finished, she asked, coldly: 'What did you want to see me about?'

'I want to ask you a favour. But maybe now isn't the right time.'

'It depends what the favour is.'

'I want to visit the teacher who came on the stage. I think her name is Miss Crane. I want to ask her some questions about what happened on the stage. But I can't call on her. I'm no longer the town marshal. On the other hand, if you'll come with me it will put the visit on a proper basis.'

'Why are you asking about Wade's death?'

'Because I've got a theory. I want to test it out.'

‘Why don’t you leave it to the proper authorities?’

‘Because Summers is an ineffective clown who can’t or won’t try to find out who killed Wade.’

She stared at him keenly. ‘You’ve got some personal axe to grind in this, haven’t you?’

‘Maybe. Are you going to help me?’

She sighed. ‘I suppose so. Anyhow I was going to call on Miss Crane as part of my duty as a church visitor — to welcome her to the town.’

They set out. They raised more than a few ladies’ eyebrows as they walked together down Main Street. Several people wondered why the attractive Cordelia should be walking with the drunkard ex-town marshal.

Miss Crane lived in a pretty cottage just outside the town. She was working in the garden when her visitors approached. She looked up from her weeding when she heard the front gate open.

‘Ah! Visitors,’ she exclaimed. ‘Just

what I need as an excuse to forget about my weeding for the time being.'

At her invitation they sat on the garden-seat while she went inside to wash her hands.

There was an awkward silence between Luke and Cordelia while they waited for her to return.

It was Luke who broke it.

'I'm sorry,' he said.

'So you should be.'

'I shouldn't have said what I said about me being a lost cause. I apologize.'

She stared at him. Eventually she gave a begrudging smile. Any further conversation was curtailed when Miss Crane returned with a tray on which were glasses of lemonade.

'I hope you like it,' she said. 'Drinking lemonade is one of my vices. As well as eating chocolate. Oh, and a few other things.'

Cordelia smiled. She explained that Luke wanted to ask her a few questions about the death of Nigel Wade.

'I'll try and help.' The teacher became serious. 'Although I don't know whether I'll be able to.'

'There's only one question. There's a suggestion that he was shot because he went for his gun,' said Luke. 'Would you have any idea whether in fact he was carrying a gun?'

'That's easy,' she replied. 'I can tell you definitely the answer to that question is no.'

'How can you be so sure?'

'Because I landed in his lap.'

Both Cordelia and Luke were puzzled.

'It happened this way,' she explained. 'We heard a shot as we were approaching Crossville. At first we didn't think anything of it. We thought it was a farmer shooting some rabbits. Then there was another shot and somebody shouted. I guess it was the leader of the outlaws. Anyhow the driver pulled up so abruptly that I ended up on the lawyer's lap. His jacket was open and I can tell you positively that he wasn't carrying a gun.'

A quarter of an hour later they left her, even though she pleaded jokingly for them to stay so that she wouldn't have to do any more weeding.

They had started to walk back towards the town when suddenly Cordelia stopped. Luke was forced to halt.

'All right, what's all this about?' she demanded, facing him.

'All what?'

'Don't play the innocent with me, Luke Tilling. We've known each other now for several years — at least long enough for me to know when you're not telling me the whole truth.'

He stared down at her. 'All right, Cordelia. You win.'

'So what are you trying to prove?'

'I'm trying to prove that the gang of outlaws who held up the stage were the same gang I was hunting when I was the town marshal. There were five of them then, and there are five of them now.'

'It could be a coincidence.'

'It's very unlikely. There aren't too many gangs of outlaws in this territory. There are a couple of others. But they've got only three members in their gangs.'

'Maybe you're right. But why are you making it a personal matter?'

'Because the leader of the gang is named Mellor. Does that name mean anything to you?'

'Wasn't he the outlaw that you saw when you let go of your daughter's hand and went for your gun.'

'That's the bastard. I'm going to hunt him down if it's the last thing I do. I've given up drinking so that my hand will be perfectly steady when I shoot him between the eyes.'

7

The following day Luke rode out to the Box O ranch. Two cowboys were standing by the large iron gate that led into the compound. Luke knew them as Townley and Yardle.

‘That’s far enough, Tilling.’ Townley had drawn his gun and was aiming it threateningly at Luke.

‘That’s what I’ve always liked about this place,’ said Luke, reining in his horse. ‘The nice friendly welcome I’ve always got here.’

‘Maybe you used to get a better welcome when you were the town marshal, but now that you’re the town drunk you’re not welcome at all,’ said Yardle.

‘How many miles is it here from the town?’ asked Luke, casually.

‘I don’t know. About six I suppose,’ answered Townley. ‘Why are you asking a stupid question like this?'

'Do you think I'd waste my time riding out here and back unless I had some important information?'

A frown creased Townley's face. In their school-days neither had shown any aptitude for learning and both were invariably at the bottom of the class.

'What information have you got?' demanded Yardle.

'That's for me to disclose and your boss to assess,' replied Luke.

'Why don't you use proper words?' demanded Townley, irritably.

'You'd better come in, I suppose,' said Yardle, ungraciously.

Luke tied up his horse and followed Yardle into the study. Gregg Oliver was seated behind a large desk. On previous occasions when Luke had visited him in his official capacity as marshal, he would have invited him to sit down. This time, however, he left him standing.

'What can I do for you, Tilling?' he demanded. He was every inch an affluent rancher, from the gold watch-chain in his waistcoat to his gold tie-pin and the two gold rings on his fingers — one of them inlaid with diamonds.

'It's about the outlaws who held up the stage a week or so back.'

'What about them?'

'I think they're the same gang of outlaws who were in the locality about a year ago. Their leader was a guy named Mellor.'

'Why are you telling me this? Do you expect me to pay you by giving you a bottle of whiskey?'

Luke kept his temper under control with an effort. Although, unseen to Oliver, his knuckles were white where he had been clenching them tightly.

'If I remember rightly they were friends of yours in the past. I was wondering whether you had seen them around lately.'

Oliver's weather-beaten face turned an interesting red.

'What are you implying, Tilling?' he snarled.

'Nothing,' replied Luke, with exaggerated innocence. 'It was just well-known that they were seen on your land at that time.'

'They might have been on my land for a short while, but I drove them off. Exactly as I'm driving you off. Now get out.' Oliver stood up to give added emphasis to his words.

While Luke was riding back to town the question kept recurring. Why should Oliver have got so hot under the collar if he had nothing to hide? He decided that maybe Wilbur could supply the answer.

'Come in, Luke,' Wilbur greeted him. 'It's always nice to see you. Although I preferred you when you took a drink,' he added, with a look of regret at the bottle of whiskey.

'I've got a job to do. I've just been to see Oliver. I reminded him that a year or so ago he was friendly with the Mellor gang. He didn't seem to want to be reminded of it.'

'I bet he didn't,' chuckled Wilbur.

'The question is why should the gang turn up in this territory after being away for a year or so? The last time I heard about them they robbed a bank in Stoneville.'

'I see you've been following their progress.'

'I read the newspapers.'

'Hm. I think I can give you the answer to your question. Maybe Oliver wanted them to persuade some of the homesteaders to fall in with his plan.'

'What plan is that?'

Wilbur explained about Bradley's visit and how the town council was insisting that the homesteaders should pay their taxes.

'I think they've got an argument if they say you must pay from now, but I don't agree with asking you for back payment,' said Luke.

'Exactly. That's why I invited Nigel here to find out the legal position. But of course he never arrived.' Wilbur choked on the last few words.

Luke waited several moments for him

to recover. Then he said: 'I've been checking up to find out exactly what happened when your nephew was killed. There's no way the outlaw could have thought he was going for his gun. The teacher said he definitely wasn't carrying one.'

Luke left shortly afterwards, after promising Wilbur that he would let him know if he found out anything further about his nephew's death. Wilbur watched him ride away. His face was a picture of sadness. If he hadn't sent for his nephew then Nigel would be alive today. He knew he would have to live with all the grief that the memory brought for the rest of his life.

8

Five men sat round a camp-fire in a clearing in the hills. Their camp was several miles outside Crossville and well off the beaten track.

'That's a hundred dollars each,' said Mellor, who had just finished sharing out the money. 'That's not bad for an hour's work.'

'It's easier than robbing a bank,' said North, his second in command.

'The four of us had a hundred dollars,' said a weasel of a man named Hitchings. 'How much did you have, boss?'

'That's between me and my maker,' snapped Mellor. He was known to his fellow outlaws to have a short fuse of a temper and wisely nobody pursued the matter.

'Now that we've come back to Crossville,' said the third member, a giant of a man named Clinker, 'What's our next step?'

'You can go into Crossville tomorrow,' said Mellor. 'Have a few drinks. Not too many, mind you. I don't want you to get drunk and start flashing your money around.'

'What are you going to do, boss?' demanded Hitchings.

'I'm going to stay here. I'm too well-known in Crossville to take the risk of going there.'

'We'll bring a couple of bottles of whiskey back,' said North.

'I don't know about spending my money on drinking, but I'm going to find a nice, shapely girl,' said the fifth member of the gang. He was a Mexican named Pedro. While the others used guns in pursuit of their illegal activities, Pedro preferred to use a knife. His aim with the throwing knife was unerring and deadly, as several opponents with whom he had come into conflict would be able to testify were they still alive.

'There's one other thing,' said

Mellor. 'I want you all to keep your ears to the ground. If you can find out any information about Luke Tilling, bring it back.'

'Luke Tilling,' said North. 'Isn't he the feller who used to be the marshal of the town?'

'That's him. He spotted me in the town the last time I was there. We both went for our guns but we weren't able to finish the fight because his daughter dashed across the road and got in the way of a horse.'

'What happened to her?' demanded Pedro.

'She was knocked down and killed.'

'The poor thing,' said Pedro, making the sign of the cross.

Mellor ignored the outlaw's protestation of grief. 'The point is that Tilling is now on my trail. According to my informant, he has been at his ranch asking questions.'

'We haven't got anything to worry about from him,' said Hitchings. 'There are five of us and only one of him.'

'Do you want us to ask around for any information about Tilling?' demanded Clinker.

'No. That's the last thing I want you to do. If you did that you'd attract attention to yourselves. Just keep your ears peeled, that's all.'

'If this Tilling is going to stir up trouble,' said North, 'why don't we just take him out?'

'That's what I'd like to do. But how?' demanded Mellor, his brow furrowed in thought.

'What does he look like?' demanded Pedro.

'Well, he's tall. Black hair. Some women would think he's handsome.'

'Just like me,' said Pedro, to general laughter.

'Yes, but his skin is a different colour,' said North.

'Tilling started hitting the bottle after his daughter was killed. But now he's sobered up. It seems his aim in life is to get even with me.'

'It's all right, boss, we'll look after

you,' said Hitchings.

Mellor aimed a kick at him but missed.

'We mustn't underestimate Tilling,' said Mellor. 'When he was the town marshal he was the best in the territory. He'll know that we are five in the gang and if he sees the four of you together it will arouse his suspicions. So I want you to go in pairs. That way if you meet him he won't be suspicious.'

'I suppose I'll have to go with this big lump,' said Pedro, pointing to Clinker.

'It's all right, little man. I'll look after you,' said Clinker, putting his arm around him.

'That leaves you and me.' Hitchings addressed the remark to North. 'We'll see what we can find out about Tilling, boss,' he added.

9

The following morning Luke's landlady, Mrs Blinkley, announced that he had a visitor. 'It's a young lady,' she added.

Luke entered the parlour half-expecting to find Cordelia there. Instead he was surprised to see that it was the teacher, Daisy Crane.

'I'm sorry about the unexpected visit,' she said. 'But I've got some information that might be of use to you.'

'There's no need to apologize. I'm always pleased to have an attractive young lady visit me.'

She smiled. 'Are you sure you haven't got any Irish blood in you, Mr Tilling?'

'Luke, please. What's this about Irish blood?'

'They are always noted for their blarney.'

'*Touché*.'

'Well, Luke I know you're interested in the outlaws who held up the stage — '

'More than interested, I'd say.'

'Yes — well, whatever your reasons. The point is I think I might be able to identify a couple of them.'

Her last statement seized Luke's interest. He leaned forward in his chair. 'Go on.'

'As you know they were all wearing masks, but while I was standing waiting for the other travellers to empty their wallets and purses, I noticed a couple of things. In the first place one of them was a big man. I mean a really big man, like a strong man in a circus. The other thing I noticed was that one of them looked like a Mexican — or at least a half-caste. He wasn't wearing a jacket and his arms were brown — not from sun-tan, it was their normal colour.'

She brushed a stray lock of hair impatiently from her forehead. Luke waited for her to continue.

'Well, I think I saw them less than a quarter of an hour ago in the town.'

'Where were they?'

'Of course I can't be one hundred per cent sure that it was them, but they were such an odd-looking couple that they caught my eye.'

'Where were they?' Luke repeated his question.

'They were going into a saloon named the Horse and Groom. I was sitting in the coffee shop opposite. I was sitting in one of the window-seats. That's how I was able to spot them.'

At that moment Mrs Blinkley came into the room.

'Can I get you two cups of coffee?' she asked.

'No thanks,' said Luke. 'We're on our way out.'

'Suit yourself,' said the landlady, rather peeved because her offer had been refused.

'Aren't you taking things for granted that I'll come with you to the café?' demanded Daisy, as Luke hurried along the street, while she kept up with him with an effort.

'These outlaws are the most dangerous men in the territory,' he replied. 'If you can help to put them behind bars it's your duty to do so.'

She glanced at him. His face was hard — he wasn't the relaxed person he had been a few minutes before.

They arrived at the café. Luckily the corner table was still vacant. They pulled up the two chairs.

After Luke had ordered coffee Daisy observed: 'Of course there's the possibility that they have left the saloon and moved on to another.'

'I doubt it. If they're camped somewhere in the hills outside the town they'll want a couple of pints of beer to quench their thirst before they decide to move on.'

'You could make sure that they're in the saloon by going inside,' suggested Daisy.

'If I did that, there's the risk that they might see me and recognize me. I was the town marshal a year or so ago. They might have seen me at that time. The last thing I want to do is to warn the gang that I'm on their trail.'

'So you don't know any of the members of the gang?'

'Only their leader, Mellor,' replied Luke, shortly.

'Yes, I heard about the unfortunate accident when you spotted him. I'm dreadfully sorry about what happened to your daughter.'

'Yeah.'

'Tragedies happen.' It was obvious to Luke that she was trying to keep her voice on an even unemotional note. But she didn't succeed.

'If you don't want to tell me about it — '

'No, it's all right. I've got over it now. It happened at the last school where I was teaching. It was the last lesson of the day. The children were copying some words from the blackboard into their books. I was staring out through the window when I saw a man walking up the path towards the school. He was a stranger. I didn't recognize him.'

Luke glanced at her. Then he quickly turned his attention back to watching the saloon.

'I went out to meet him. I wanted to tell him that only teachers and officials were allowed on the school premises. He was a middle-aged man. He was puffing slightly. The school was built on a hill and it was quite a steep climb to get to it.

'I stood by the door and when he came up to me I asked him what he wanted. He said he was looking for a boy named Fineburg. There were only two classes in the school and I knew the names of every one of the pupils. I knew there was nobody named Fineburg.

'I told him so. He asked if I could do him a favour. Could I give him a glass of water. I don't know how to explain this, but there was something about him that wasn't quite right. He was wearing a blue suit and looked like some kind of office worker. But he wasn't wearing a tie — if he had been working in an office he would have been wearing a tie. I also noticed that he was wearing black shoes which didn't look as though they had been polished for ages. As I said he was puffing, having come up the slope, and he was perspiring.'

She paused. Luke again shot her a quick glance.

After a few moments she continued: 'It was always school policy not to let anyone on the premises who wasn't a parent of one of the children. This was drummed into me from the day I accepted the teaching post. He was standing in front of me. He had large brown eyes. They reminded me of a spaniel's I once had. I knew I should tell him that he wasn't allowed inside the school. Instead I broke the rules and led him inside the classroom. I told him he could sit down while I fetched him a glass of water. Do you know what happened next?' She choked on the question.

'No.'

'While I was in the kitchen fetching the water he took out his two revolvers and emptied the chambers aiming at the children. The last bullet he kept for himself. When I came back there were eight dead children in the classroom. Three were seriously injured and they died from their wounds shortly afterwards.'

'You weren't to know that he was a lunatic.' This time Luke glanced long and hard at her before resuming his watch on the saloon.

'I had a gun in the house. It was my father's who fought in the Civil War. For days afterwards I thought about taking my own life. After all, I had been responsible for the children and I abdicated that responsibility. As a result eleven were dead. I never had enough courage to take my own life.'

'You can't blame yourself for what was an act of kindness.'

'No. But the people in the town blamed me,' she said, bitterly. 'I could see it in their eyes every time they passed me in the street. It eventually came too much to bear. I had a mental breakdown. When I recovered I knew I had to move on to another town.'

She took out a handkerchief and blew her nose energetically.

'You'll start a new life here,' stated Luke, reassuringly. 'Does anyone else know about your tragedy?'

'No. I suppose I only told you because you've suffered a loss yourself.'

'Yes. Maybe it would have been better if I'd had a mental breakdown. Instead I took to the bottle.'

'I know. I heard. But you're over it now, aren't you?'

'Yes, I'm over it,' said Luke, positively.

At that moment two men came out of the saloon. One was a large man who fitted Daisy's description of a strong man in a circus. The other was a slight figure — a Mexican.

‘It’s them,’ Daisy whispered, excitedly.

Luke studied them as they stood by the door of the saloon waiting for a carriage to pass before they could cross the road. Daisy couldn’t contain her excitement. She gripped his hand.

At that moment Cordelia entered the café. She glanced around and saw Luke and Daisy. To all intents and purposes Daisy was holding Luke’s hand.

‘I was going to have a cup of coffee with you,’ snapped Cordelia, addressing Luke. ‘But I see you’re otherwise engaged.’ With that she flounced out of the café.

10

Half an hour later Luke called at the marshal's office. Summers was inside studying a report.

'What can I do for you?' the marshal demanded, in tones which were markedly less than friendly.

'I've got some information about the outlaws who attacked the stage a couple of weeks ago.'

'I suppose you'd better sit down,' said Summers, grudgingly. 'Right, let's hear what you've got.'

'The new teacher, Miss Crane, has identified two of the men.'

'How could she do that? They were wearing masks.'

'One of them was a big man. A very big man. She describes him as like a circus strong man.'

'So? There are probably several people in Crossville who would fit that description.'

'But there was also another outlaw — a small man. He was obviously a Mexican.'

'Go on.'

'Miss Crane spotted the two of them going into the Horse and Groom saloon.'

'Why didn't she come to tell me?'

'She told me because she knew that I've got an interest in the case.'

'Well anyhow, I think the evidence is very slim. According to my information the Mellor gang have been spotted over a hundred miles away in Almington.'

'Well, I think that information is wrong.' Luke was beginning to get angry. 'Just as your theory is wrong about the outlaw thinking that Wade was going for his gun.'

'You've got to admit it's a possibility.' Summers was now on the defensive.

'It's not even a possibility,' Luke snapped. 'Miss Crane can definitely vouch for the fact that Wade wasn't carrying a gun.'

'Miss Crane seems to know a lot

about this case,' snapped the marshal, testily.

'So the fact that Wade's murder was premeditated raises some interesting questions.'

'I'll look into it,' stated the marshal. 'Now if you'll excuse me, I've got some work to catch up with.' He turned his attention again to the report he had been reading.

'I'll just have a look through the rogue's gallery,' said Luke. He was referring to the collection of drawings of known criminals on the wall. Most of them carried a price for their capture dead or alive. Luke spent several minutes searching for a large man who could be strong man in a circus and a small Mexican. He could find neither.

'Mellor's picture used to be up here,' he stated.

'My deputy has been clearing out some of the old pictures,' stated Summers.

'There used to be a reward for

capturing him. It was five hundred dollars.'

'Are you thinking of becoming a bounty hunter?' sneered the marshal.

'Maybe,' said Luke. 'I sat in that chair for a few years and I'd get more for shooting Mellor and his gang than I was paid during that time.'

'If you want to catch him you'd better go to Almington,' advised the marshal.

'I think the answer is here. In Crossville,' said Luke, stubbornly.

'Look, Luke, the person who shot the lawyer could have made a mistake. He could have thought that he was carrying a gun. That's why he shot him,' said the marshal, with another attempt at reasonableness.

'According to Miss Crane the lawyer was wearing a jacket which was open. Mellor would have been able to see that he wasn't carrying a gun. No, it was deliberate, premeditated murder.'

'Well, whichever way it happened I'm convinced the gang of outlaws are far enough away. I've sent a telegram to the marshal in Almington asking him if he's got any more information about the gang.'

'And if I've got any more information I'll pass it on,' Luke said, as he headed for the door.

'Thanks,' said Summers, without looking up from his report.

However when he was sure that Luke had left the office he opened the drawer of his desk and drew out the drawings of five outlaws. He studied two of them carefully.

'So Miss Crane saw you two,' he said, as he studied the drawings of Clinker and Pedro. 'That can only mean one thing. Tilling is right in thinking that you are still in the vicinity.'

11

When Cordelia returned to the church house her father could see that she was visibly upset. He wisely refrained from asking her directly the cause. Shortly afterwards help arrived in the form of the curate, Padlow.

'I'm thinking of taking the morning air,' he announced. 'Would you care to walk with me, Cordelia?'

She was about to make some excuse not to accompany him, when she suddenly changed her mind.

'Just wait until I get my bonnet and I'll be ready.'

As they were walking along Main Street several pedestrians stopped to wish them good-morning.

'You seem very popular in the town, Cordelia,' observed Padlow.

'I grew up here, so most of the people know me,' she replied. 'Although of course a lot of strangers have come into the town recently.'

'I hope you're not referring to me as one of the strangers. My fervent hope is that we will become better acquainted.'

What did he mean by that, she wondered. However her thoughts were interrupted by the sight of Luke coming out of the marshal's office. He was obviously surprised at seeing the two of them together.

Cordelia smiled sweetly at him as they passed. Luke scowled in the direction of Padlow.

'If I may say so, Cordelia, I don't think your association with the town drunk is a healthy one.'

'He's not the town drunk,' she flared up. 'He's given up drinking.'

'I hope you're right.'

'And anyhow it's none of your business whom I associate with.'

'I know I have no legal connection with your family at this moment. But perhaps it's not too much for me to hope that at some time in the future that position might change.'

Again Cordelia was puzzled by his remark. Then, when they walked a short distance the thought struck her like a bombshell. The curate by her side was thinking that there might be a romantic attachment between them at some future date. Oh, no! She stopped in her tracks.

'Are you all right, Cordelia?' Padlow enquired, solicitously.

'I'm afraid I've just remembered something. I've got to go back to the house. There's some urgent church business to attend to.'

'I'll come back with you.'

'No, it's all right. You carry on enjoying your walk.'

She turned on her heel and started hurrying back before he could join her.

⋆ ⋆ ⋆

Later in the afternoon Clinker and Pedro returned to the outlaws' camp.

North and Hitchings had already returned.

'It took you two a long time to get back here,' said Mellor.

'I'm afraid I was unavoidably detained,' said Pedro. 'You should have seen her. She must have been the most shapely *señorita* in Crossville.'

Clinker was unloading the provisions he had brought with him.

'I've brought some bottles of whiskey,' he announced.

'That's good,' said Mellor. 'It gets cold here in the hills at night.'

'We've also got some news,' said Pedro.

'What is it?' said Mellor, who had opened a bottle of whiskey and was drinking from it.

'It's about the young lady who was on the stage.'

'What about her?' said Mellor, wiping his mouth with his sleeve.

'She spotted us.'

'What do you mean, she spotted you?'

'She was sitting in the window in the café next to the saloon that we went into.'

'But how could she have spotted you?' demanded North. 'We were all wearing masks.'

'She probably recognized us because I'm a big guy and he's a little guy,' said Clinker.

'And because I'm a Mex,' supplied Pedro.

'You could be mistaken,' suggested Hitchings.

'No, by the time we came out somebody had joined her. We could see that they were watching the saloon, even though they pretended they weren't.'

'Who had joined her?' demanded Mellor, although he felt that he already knew the answer.

'It was the guy you described,' said Pedro. 'I think it was Tilling.'

Mellor took his bottle of whiskey and carried it a short distance away from the others. He was obviously deep in thought and the outlaws knew that it would not be advisable to interrupt his meditations.

At last he came to a conclusion.

'I'm going into town,' he announced.

'But isn't there a danger that you might get recognized?' asked North.

'It'll be getting dark by the time I get there. There shouldn't be any danger of being recognized.'

'Do you want any of us to come with you, boss?' asked Hitchings.

'No, it's all right. This is something I've got to do on my own.'

The others wisely didn't ask what the 'something' was.

12

The following morning Wilbur and the homesteaders were holding a meeting. The fact that they were holding it in the morning when they were usually working out in their fields showed how important it was.

Wilbur started to count the number of homesteaders who were present. Tom Mullings said: 'There's no need to count us, Wilbur. We're all present.'

'All except the six Judases, I suppose,' snapped Wilbur.

'I think it's a bit strong to call them that,' said a Dane named Jorgens. 'If they want to go into debt to Oliver, it's up to them.'

'Most of us have been here for several years,' said Wilbur. 'We've always helped each other out. When somebody had been ill at harvest time and wasn't able to get his crops in, we'd all help out. We've all been like one family —'

'A big family, I'd say,' said a small wiry man named Dyke. 'I've got nine kids of my own.'

The others laughed.

At least they're all in a good, friendly mood, thought Wilbur. Let's hope they'll stay like that when we come to the end of the meeting.

'I know I'm speaking for all of us when I say that we were all shocked to hear about the death of your nephew,' said Jorgens.

'Murder, you mean,' snapped Wilbur.

'I thought he was shot because the outlaw thought he was reaching for his gun,' said a sandy-haired Scotsman named McCloud.

'Luke Tilling has been here. He's investigating the case,' said Wilbur. 'He's found out that the outlaw must have seen that my nephew wasn't carrying a gun.'

'I thought Luke Tilling was the town drunk,' said Dooney, a comparative newcomer among the homesteaders.

'He's given up drinking,' said Wilbur, shortly.

'I wish I could,' said Dyke, holding up the half-empty glass of the whiskey with which Wilbur had supplied them when they had come into the house.

The others laughed.

Now's the time to broach the subject thought Wilbur. Aloud he said: 'I think Oliver is going to use the collection of taxes as an excuse to get rid of us.'

There was silence while the others digested the startling suggestion. At last Jorgens said: 'How can he get rid of us? The government said the land is ours. I've got a document to prove it.'

'Yes, but only as long as you don't break the law. If you should be caught stealing, for example, then your land could be forfeit.'

'We understand that,' said McCloud, irritably. 'We've all stayed on the right side of the law for the past seven years and I can't see anybody breaking it now.'

'But you will be if you refuse to pay

the taxes,' said Wilbur, playing his trump card.

'You mean they can turn us off our land if we don't pay the two hundred and eighty dollars?' said a shocked Dyke.

'I've been to see the marshal, and that's what he says,' said Wilbur. 'That's why I sent for my nephew — to find out the exact legal position. But of course he never arrived.' He tried in vain to conceal his bitterness.

'So what do you suggest we do?' demanded Mullings.

'The first thing we've got to do is to stick together. It's worked for us in the past and it will help us again,' said Wilbur.

'What about paying the tax?' demanded McCloud.

'I don't see how we can get out of paying the forty dollars for this year,' said Wilbur. 'Even though we don't use the town's water supply, some of you send your children to the school and the teacher's got to be paid.'

'Yes, I definitely use that part of the town's finances,' said Dyke, to general laughter.

'So we pay the forty dollars and hope that the town council will forget about the back payment,' suggested Mullings.

'I'm going to see Bradley and tell him that that's how far we are prepared to go,' said Wilbur.

'You'd better start eating humble-pie now, after what you did to him the last time he called here,' advised a tall, thin homesteader named Lawson.

There was general laughter.

'Whatever happens I think there's one other thing we should do,' stated Wilbur.

'What's that?' demanded McCloud.

'We should prepare for a show of strength.'

'How do you mean?' demanded Dyke.

'We've all got rifles. I suggest you make sure that they're in good working order. And make sure you've got plenty of bullets.'

'I'm not going to shoot anybody,' said McCloud, with alarm. 'I only use my rifle to shoot rabbits and wild pigs.'

'It's a game of bluff,' said Wilbur. 'None of us intends shooting anybody. But if we show Bradley and the councillors that we're willing to fight for our rights, the chances are that they'll back down about the idea of collecting back taxes.'

While they mulled over Wilbur's suggestion, Lawson voiced their fears. 'I hope it *is* just a game of bluff,' he said, fervently.

13

Later in the day Luke was seated in the coffee-house. He was in the window-seat where he could watch the passers-by. He was searching for a certain face among the women who were strolling along the sidewalk. At last he spotted the one he was watching out for. When she came past the window, he tapped on it to attract her attention.

Cordelia glanced in his direction. When she saw who had attracted her attention she deliberately held her head high and prepared to walk past. Luke tapped on the window, this time more insistently. She glanced in his direction for a second time. Luke put his hands together in the universally recognized gesture of supplication. Cordelia smiled.

When she came in she asked: 'Did you want to see me?'

'I've got some explaining to do.

Would you like a cup of coffee?'

After a moment's hesitation she agreed.

When their coffee arrived she said: 'Now what's this explanation?'

'When you saw Daisy holding my hand it wasn't what you might have assumed it was.'

'I didn't assume anything,' she said, coldly.

'We came here because she thought she had spotted two of the outlaws who attacked the stage.'

'Where were they? In here?' she demanded, puzzled.

'No. They'd gone into the saloon next door. We were waiting for them to come out.'

'And so you held hands while you were waiting.'

'You know sometimes I think your father slipped up in not giving you a good spanking when you were younger.'

'Any time you want to remedy it, you are quite welcome to try,' she replied, icily.

Luke sighed. 'Well anyhow, Daisy spotted the outlaws coming out of the saloon.'

'So you'd recognize them if you saw them again?'

'Yes. One was a big guy. The other was a Mexican.'

'I don't understand. How did she recognize them? I thought they were wearing masks when they held up the stage.'

'They were. But there aren't many guys the size of this outlaw. And there aren't many Mexicans in Crossville — we're too far north.'

'Did you tell the marshal about this?'

'Yes. You saw me coming out of the marshal's office when you were out walking with your paramour.'

'He isn't my . . . ' she began, then realized from his expression that he had trapped her into the confession. 'Very funny,' she snapped.

A few moments later she finished her coffee and stood up.

'Don't go,' said Luke.

'Why? Have you any more information about the outlaws?'

'No. But I want to ask you a favour.'

'Ask away. There's no guarantee though that I'll grant it.'

'Will you come to Daisy's cottage with me? You know what this town is like. You know how tongues will start wagging if I visit her on my own.'

'I don't see why I should help you after your comments about me not having had a good spanking.'

A couple of elderly ladies who were seated at the next table glanced at Cordelia with interest when they overheard the last remark.

'I'm sorry. I take the remark back,' said a contrite Luke.

'Oh, all right. I'll come with you. I've got a couple of calls myself to make out in that direction.'

They set off down Main Street. Some heads turned to watch them.

'They say he's given up drinking,' said one of the ladies on the sidewalk.

'They make a handsome couple,' said another.

'It isn't Luke Tilling she's set her sights on,' said a third.

'Who is it, then?'

'The curate. Padlow.'

'Padlow? Well I never.'

'They were out walking together yesterday. Padlow told Mrs Lewis — the lady who cleans the church — that he has expectations that he and Cordelia will become good friends.'

'Or more than just good friends,' suggested the other.

Luke and Cordelia reached Daisy's cottage. Neither had spoken during their walk. Daisy wasn't working in the garden as she had been on their previous visit.

Luke knocked at the door. Cordelia sat on the garden seat while she waited for Daisy to answer.

It was obvious after a few minutes that in fact there wasn't going to be an answer.

'She's not in,' said Cordelia.

'She's left the door unlocked,' said Luke. He pushed it gently and it swung open.

'She must have forgotten to lock it.'

Luke called out: 'Miss Crane.'

There was no reply.

'You stay here,' Luke said. 'I'm going to make sure that she isn't in.'

He went into the living-room. It was empty. The kitchen door was open. He hesitated before going inside. The sight that met his eyes caused him to cry out 'Oh, God!'

'What is it? What's the matter?' Cordelia had materialized by his side. She screamed when she saw the cause of Luke's utterance.

Daisy was lying on the floor. She was lying in a pool of her blood, the result of somebody cutting her throat. Cordelia did what any respectable young lady would have done who had never seen such a horrible sight. She fainted.

14

Wilbur was sitting in Bradley's office. Wilbur was impressed by the office fittings, from the solid oak desk to the thick woollen carpet on the floor. He couldn't help but contrast it with the carpet in his living-room, which consisted of sacking into which he had painstakingly pushed hundreds of small strips of cloth to make the carpet.

'What can I do for you, Mr Daniels?' asked Bradley. He was seated behind the desk and to Wilbur's jaundiced eye the question wasn't without a certain amount of unfriendliness in its tone.

'I've come to see you about payment of the council taxes,' replied Wilbur.

'Ah!' Bradley rubbed his hands. 'You've seen sense at last.'

'In a way. First I would like to apologize for my behaviour when you visited my farm a couple of weeks back.'

'Thanks. We'll let bygones be bygones, shall we?'

'At least now you've learned what slurry is,' said Wilbur.

If he was expecting even a half-sympathetic acknowledgement of the fact from Bradley, he was mistaken. All he received in response was a frown.

Wilbur cleared his throat. 'Most of the homesteaders have held a meeting and we've come to a conclusion.'

'I'm listening.'

'We've agreed to pay this year's taxes. Forty dollars.'

'And?'

'That's it.'

'What about the back payments?'

'We don't see that we should pay them. As you know, my nephew, who was a lawyer, was coming here to argue our case. Unfortunately he was shot before he was in a position to do so.' Wilbur who had been successfully trying to keep calm, suddenly choked on the last sentence.

'I'm sorry about your nephew. But it doesn't alter the fact that you and the other homesteaders owe back taxes of two hundred and eighty dollars each.'

'We're not going to pay it.' Wilbur not only shouted but emphasized the point by thumping on Bradley's desk.

'I'm afraid it's the law. If you don't pay you'll be in contempt and liable to be evicted from your land.'

'Who's going to evict me?' growled Wilbur.

'That's up to the marshal. No doubt he'll get a body of men together.'

'He'll evict me over my dead body.' Wilbur, who had stood up, was shouting loudly.

Bradley, who had kept calm during the discussion now began to show signs of trepidation. He remembered how Wilbur had thrown his shoes out of his house. Here was a man with an uncontrollable temper. It was difficult to guess how far he would go if pushed to the limit. Was he carrying a gun?

Bradley's blood iced at the thought.

'It's not my decision. I'm the person who carries the messages.'

'You're the one who does their dirty work,' Wilbur spat out.

'Yes, I suppose you could say that.' The last thing Bradley was going to do at present was argue with him. He had observed the way Wilbur's face had reddened and how he was clenching and unclenching his fists. Somebody in one of the other offices had told him that Wilbur was an ex-Indian fighter. That he had killed dozens of Indians while he was in the army. Bradley suddenly realized that his mouth had become dry.

'Well, you can tell whoever comes to try to evict us that we'll be ready.'

'Wha . . . at do you mean?'

Wilbur leaned forward and put his hand on the desk. Bradley took an involuntary step backwards.

'What is an essential part of a homesteader's equipment, Mr Bradley?'

Bradley hesitated. 'A plough?'

'Think again?'

There was still menace in Wilbur's attitude. Bradley had stepped back and could now go no further since he was up against the wall. He licked his lips.

'A scythe,' he suggested, hopefully.

'A gun, Mr Bradley. A gun.' Wilbur emphasized the statement by thumping on the desk.

'You wouldn't fight the law.' Disbelief and incredulity stretched Bradley's tones. In his eyes the law was sacrosanct. Even to think about breaking it was on a par with treason.

'I'll fight for what's mine. I've sweated and toiled for seven years to get that farm to the state, it is. I've worked all the daylight hours God could send and often late into the night. I've looked after my livestock and nursed them as lovingly as any mother with her baby. That's something you town people will never understand. What I'm saying is that that land is mine. I've got a document to prove it. And God help anybody who tries to take it away from me.'

Wilbur stormed out of the office, banging the door so hard that after Bradley had allowed a reasonable time to elapse, when he went he over to close it he automatically checked to see whether its hinges had been damaged.

15

When Cordelia opened her eyes, for a moment she couldn't take in her surroundings. Then realization flooded back.

'Take it easy,' Luke advised.

She was lying on the garden-seat where he had carried her after she had fainted. She shook her head as if to try to clear it of the horrible picture which she had witnessed.

'I've sent the young boy next door to fetch the marshal,' said Luke. 'He should be here soon.'

'Who would do such a terrible thing?' asked Cordelia, knowing she wouldn't receive an answer.

The neighbour came out to see whether she had recovered. 'I'll bring the poor thing a glass of water. Unless she wants something stronger.'

'Water will be fine,' Luke assured her.

'What's happening to this town?' demanded Cordelia, after accepting the glass of water. 'First the lawyer was shot, now the teacher. Does the fact that they were both on the stage have something to do with their killings?'

'I don't know,' confessed Luke.

'You're the expert. You're the detective. You should know.'

'I don't see how it can be anything to do with their both being on the stage.'

'We haven't had a murder in the town for a couple of years. And now we've had two in a couple of weeks.'

Any further discussion was interrupted by the arrival of the marshal.

'I hear you've found a body,' said Summers.

'Is that all you can say?' cried Cordelia. 'I hear you've found a body. There's a poor girl in there who until a few hours ago was a vibrant living person. She was a person who breathed the same air that you're breathing now. Doesn't that make you want to weep?'

'I've got my job to do,' snapped the

marshal. He went into the cottage and Luke followed him.

The marshal went through the living-room and into the kitchen. He glanced down at the corpse.

'She's been dead for some hours,' stated Luke.

Summers touched her cheek.

'Yes, she's stone cold.'

'She must have been killed by somebody she knew.'

'How do you make that out?'

'She was killed here, not in the living-room. She was probably going to make a cup of coffee for the killer.'

'It's a theory,' said Summers, dismissively.

'It's more than a theory. It's a probability. There are two coffee cups on the side-table. She would have got the cups down from the cupboard ready to carry them into the living-room.'

'I'll give you another theory,' said Summers. 'Somebody could have knocked at the door. When she opened it, this guy could have been holding a gun. He could have said: Go back into the house — into the kitchen. Then he could have taken one of the knives from the drawer and cut her throat.'

'It doesn't explain the two cups on the table.'

'Maybe they had nothing to do with the murderer. She might have had a visitor beforehand. She might have washed up the cups and just left them on the table.'

There was the sound of a horse drawing up. A few moments later the doctor entered.

Doc Gribble was middle-aged. He had been an army doctor before settling down in Crossville. He had seen hundreds of dead bodies, nevertheless he gave an exclamation of horror on seeing the corpse.

'Who'd do a thing like this?' he demanded, as he knelt down by the corpse.

'That's what I'd like to know,' said

Summers. 'If I find him I'll hang him in the square.'

'She's been dead for over twelve hours,' the doctor announced.

'Could she have been dead for, say, twenty-four hours?' asked Luke.

'It's possible. It's always difficult to tell the time of death once the corpse has started stiffening up.'

'What difference does it make, what time she died?' demanded Summers, irritably.

'Say she died yesterday evening. There are five cottages in this row. It's possible that one of the neighbours might have seen the murderer arrive.'

'Yes, it's worth looking into,' concurred the doctor.

'I'll visit them myself,' snapped Summers. 'I want you to remember, Tilling, that you've no part in this investigation. In fact I'd like you out of here, now.'

Luke went out. There was no sign of Cordelia on the garden seat.

'If you're looking for the preacher's

daughter, she's in our house,' said the boy Luke had sent to get the marshal.

In fact she was in the cottage being encouraged to drink some warm broth by the boy's mother.

'I was telling her this is one of the best things you can have for a case of shock,' explained the neighbour.

Cordelia gave Luke a wan smile. 'Mrs Voyle here has been very kind.'

'Nonsense, my dear. You've had a shock. A big shock. To think of that poor girl lying there for ages and we didn't know anything about it.'

'Did somebody call there yesterday evening?' demanded Luke.

'I'm not sure. I can't see the front door from our living-room. I think, however, that I heard a horse. I wouldn't be able to see that either because the hedge is in the way.'

'Have you any idea what time it might have been?'

'I'm afraid I don't keep track of the time. Only when I'm waiting for our youngest to come home from school.'

Cordelia stood up. 'Thanks for the broth.'

'You're welcome, dear. I'll ask my Henry if he heard anybody calling to see the teacher. He won't be in for a couple of hours. But you never know — he might have heard something.'

Luke and Cordelia left. Cordelia put her arm in his as they walked down the road.

'They're a lovely-looking couple,' Mrs Voyle said to herself, as she went into the kitchen to wash up the dishes.

16

Daisy's funeral was as well-attended as Nigel Wade's had been. Luke heard the often repeated remark: *to think that two people have been murdered in the town in less than a fortnight*.

The Reverend Dance again allowed Padlow to conduct a part of the service. Padlow waxed lyrical about Daisy's virtues and the fact that she had chosen to come to Crossville when she could obviously have chosen any other town.

'What did we do?' he roared. 'We snatched her young life from her. We threw her love for the town back in her face. It is something which will haunt us for the rest of our lives. While Daisy is up there with the angels looking down on us, I hope she will forgive us . . . '

He carried on for another quarter of an hour in the same vein.

'Why did you give him a chance to preach?' Cordelia whispered to her father when Padlow showed signs of at last coming to the end of his sermon.

'He's a part of the community now,' said her father. 'And anyhow he wants to impress you.'

'What do you mean?'

'He's told me that he wants you and him to become good friends. Or even more than just good friends.'

'Over my dead body,' snapped Cordelia.

Later, when she and Luke were seated at their usual window-seat in the coffee-house, Cordelia asked 'Why *did* Daisy come to the town? Do you know?'

'I suppose she was trying to forget.'

'What do you mean?'

'She told me about an incident which happened in the last town where she was teaching.' Luke went on to describe how Daisy had allowed a man into the school under the pretext that he wanted a glass of water. Then when she went to fetch the water he started shooting the children. Finally he shot himself.

'Oh, how terrible,' cried Cordelia.

'He was obviously some kind of lunatic,' stated Luke.

'Yet he must have appeared to be a normal person, otherwise she would never have let him into the school.'

'I suppose so.'

'Do you think that the person behind these killings could be some kind of lunatic?'

'Maybe. Although I still think that Daisy knew the killer and invited him into her house.'

Cordelia shivered. 'So there could be somebody in the town, who to all intents and purposes is leading a normal life, who could be a crazy killer?'

'It's just a theory,' said Luke, trying to reassure her. 'When I was marshal I never came across anybody who killed without having a good reason.'

A young man approached their table. 'Excuse me,' he said. 'I'm Daisy's brother. You might have seen me at the funeral. I was hoping that somebody could explain why she was killed. Somebody at the funeral pointed you out to me.' He indicated Luke.

Luke introduced himself and Cordelia. 'Why don't you sit down,' suggested Luke.

'By the way, my name is Stephen Crane.'

Luke ordered coffees. When they arrived he began to put Stephen in the picture regarding his sister's death. At the end of Luke's description Stephen said: 'So you've no idea why she was murdered?' He couldn't conceal the disappointment in his voice.

'I'm afraid not.'

'One theory is that there might be a lunatic at large in the town,' suggested Cordelia.

'If so that would be ironic,' said Stephen.

'How do you mean?' demanded Luke, although he felt that he already knew the answer.

'It was a lunatic who was responsible for her coming to the town in the first place. I suppose you know about that?'

'Yes,' replied Cordelia.

'She always said that she should have been killed along with the children. She felt responsible for what he did. Now, to come here and be killed by a lunatic — if that's what happened — would have been the ultimate irony.'

Cordelia invited Stephen to her house. 'I'm sure that my father, the preacher, would like to meet you.'

Stephen accepted. When the two stood up to leave, Luke asked: 'By the way, Stephen, what is your occupation? You're not a lawyer by any chance?'

'No, I'm a writer. I'm a newspaper reporter. Why did you want to know whether I'm a lawyer?'

'That's another story,' replied Luke, ignoring Cordelia's frown of disapproval.

17

After the funeral some of the homesteaders returned to Wilbur's farm. When he had seen that they were all supplied with full glasses of whiskey, Wilbur said:

'It's my sad duty to propose a toast. To the unfortunate people who were on the stage a couple of weeks back and who have since met their death in violent circumstances. To Nigel Wade and Daisy Crane.'

They all raised their glasses.

'Do you think their killing has got anything to do with the fact that they were both on the stage?' demanded Mullings.

'I don't know. I've been thinking it over. The more you think about it, the less sense it makes. I could see why Oliver should have my nephew killed — '

'You think he's behind it all?' demanded Dooney.

'I'm sure he is,' stated Wilbur, with complete conviction.

'But what about the teacher? Where does she fit in?' asked Dyke.

'That's the problem. Where *does* she fit in?'

'There's some more bad news,' stated Mullings. He hadn't intended to mention the subject so early in the meeting. But having had a few drinks of Wilbur's whiskey he found the strength.

'What is it?' demanded Wilbur.

'Three of the homesteaders have left.'

'Left?' yelled Wilbur.

'They decided they can't run their farms if they get rid of some of their stock to pay the taxes. So Oliver bought them out. I was talking to one of them, Stan Wilson. He said that Oliver had offered him a good deal.'

Wilbur's face was a picture. It was purple and bursting with anger.

'Have another drink,' suggested Mullings, taking Wilbur's glass from his hand and pouring another generous measure into it.

'I'll bet Oliver gave them a good deal,' snarled Wilbur. 'But if any of you went to ask him for the same deal you wouldn't get it. He'll pay less and less now that he knows he's got us over a barrel.'

'I helped Dayton pack up his belongings,' said McCloud. 'His wife was so upset she couldn't stop crying.'

'The bastard.' Wilbur slammed his fist down on the table.

'What do we do now?' demanded Dyke.

'I'll go and see Oliver tomorrow. I'll tell him that none of us are going to move from our farms. Is that agreed?'

There was a chorus of agreement.

'I'll tell him what I've already told Bradley, that I'm willing to fight for what is mine.'

There was another chorus of agreement. Whether as a result of Wilbur's whiskey, it would be difficult to determine — but this one was even louder than the first.

'I'll let you all know the result of my meeting,' said Wilbur. Shortly afterwards the others began to disperse. There was no doubt that their predominant mood was one of anger. Several spoke about checking their rifles. The statements brought a wry smile from Wilbur.

* * *

The following day Wilbur rode out to the Box O ranch. He was met by the two cowboys, Townley and Yardle, who were guarding the gate.

'That's far enough, Wilbur.' Townley was pointing his gun at the new arrival.

'Tell your boss I want to see him,' snapped Wilbur.

While Yardle disappeared inside the ranch Wilbur sat immobile on his horse. Townley became distinctly uncomfortable under Wilbur's prolonged gaze. He was patently relieved when his companion returned and announced that Mr

Oliver would see him.

Wilbur was shown into the study. He had been there on at least a couple of occasions previously but he was still impressed by the mahogany bookcase with its collection of rare books — some of them in vellum, which he guessed must be worth a fortune.

'Do you like old books?' asked Oliver, seeing Wilbur's admiring glance in their direction.

'I'd like to have more time to read books.'

'You could. If you accept the generous terms I'm offering for your farm.'

'I'm a farmer. I work with my hands. If I had the time to sit down every day and read a book I'd soon be bored to death.'

'I assume you haven't come here to talk about books?'

'No, I haven't.' Wilbur's tone hardened. 'I've come to tell you to stop buying out the homesteaders.'

Oliver smiled. 'And by what God-given right do you stand to make that statement?'

'By the right that we own our land. It was given to us by the government. Nobody can take it away.'

'I agree. But there's nothing stopping any of the homesteaders from signing that right away. Particularly if they're offered a fair price for the land.'

'None of this would have happened in the first place if the town council hadn't claimed that we owe them taxes.'

Oliver shrugged. 'That's up to the town council. I've offered to lend the homesteaders money to pay their taxes. A few have accepted. I can offer you the same deal.'

'Over my dead body,' snarled Wilbur.

'In that case I don't see that we've anything more to discuss.'

'I'd just like to make this clear.' Wilbur was shouting. 'We've all agreed to fight you. You're not going to pick us off one by one. We're going to defend what is ours.'

'I've heard some of you have been busy practising your rifle shooting,' said Oliver, drily.

'I don't need to practise,' snapped Wilbur. 'I can still hit a jack rabbit at three hundred paces.'

'I have no doubt that you can. But I think this discussion is getting a bit pointless.'

'We've been here now for seven years. You've always wanted to take over our land. But until now you haven't had a chance. But now you've seized your chance by having my nephew killed in the first place — '

'How dare you accuse me of that.' Oliver had stood up and was also shouting.

'We'll find the proof. It doesn't matter how many years it takes. I'm sure that Luke Tilling will turn up something.'

At the mention of Luke's name Oliver sat down. Wilbur took some degree of satisfaction from the fact that Oliver was no longer standing facing him.

'Luke will keep on digging, you can be sure of that.'

'Get out,' yelled Oliver.

'I'm going. But don't think you've heard the last of our efforts to find out the truth about my nephew's murder.'

As he rode away from the ranch the thought kept pounding in Wilbur's head. *He does know something about Nigel's death.*

18

A couple of days later Luke called at the church house. Padlow opened the door. 'Good morning. Is Cordelia in?' Luke enquired.

'I'll see whether Miss Dance is free,' Padlow replied, coldly.

A couple of minutes later Cordelia herself came to the door. 'Come in, Luke,' she greeted him warmly.

He was shown into the parlour. 'To what do I owe this call so early in the morning?' she enquired.

'It's always nice to see a pretty face. It cheers me up for the rest of the day.'

She smiled. 'I suppose you think that flattery will get you a cup of coffee.'

'It will help. Especially since I'm going away for a few days.'

'Where to?' There was concern in her voice.

'Chicago.'

‘Chicago?’

‘There’s a business matter and a personal matter that I’ve got to sort out.’

‘I see.’ She went into the kitchen to make the coffee. Luke stared aimlessly out through the window.

‘I might as well tell you about the business matter,’ he said, when she returned.

‘Has it got something to do with the two murders?’

‘You always could read my mind. Yes, I suppose it has.’

‘Well?’

‘When I was town marshal I had some dealings with a lawyer in Chicago named Chiddlehurst.’

‘And?’

‘I’m going to see him while I’m there to find out the exact legal position about whether they can force Wilbur and the rest of the homesteaders to pay their back taxes.’

‘Yes, it would be nice to have the legal position defined once and for all.’

She sipped her coffee thoughtfully.

'There's one other thing. I'll be away for a few days . . .'

'Yes, it's bound to take you a few days to get to Chicago and back.'

'I don't want to alarm you, but I don't think you should go about on your own visiting the sick and needy until these murders have been solved.'

'I see.'

'It's just a sensible precaution, that's all.'

'So what do you suggest? That I stay in the house until the murders are solved — if they ever get solved.'

'Not necessarily. What about asking Padlow to accompany you. The two of you were walking out together a few days ago.'

Cordelia grimaced at the mention of Padlow's name. 'Do I have to have him with me?'

'It's a sensible precaution. Believe me.'

'Oh, all right,' she said, with resignation.

'Without being alarmist I think Crossville has become a dangerous town. Especially after Daisy's murder. I called to see Summers yesterday and pointed that out to him. I asked him to take on at least one extra deputy — but he refused.'

'Perhaps if Father had a word with him — that might help?'

'That's a good idea. Tell him to impress on Summers the need to have a deputy walking around the town where folks can see him. It will help to restore confidence in law and order.'

At that moment there was a knock at the door. Cordelia called out 'come in', and Padlow entered.

'Don't forget we have to arrange the order of the service tomorrow, Cordelia,' he said, ignoring Luke.

'Padlow, can you use a gun?' demanded Luke.

'A gun? What sort of gun?'

'A revolver. Like this.' Luke pushed aside his coat, revealing his own gun. He then proceeded to draw it with startling rapidity.

Padlow took a startled step backwards. 'I don't think that's the sort of thing to produce in a house belonging to God,' he squeaked.

'I take it that means you don't carry one,' said Luke, drily.

'Luke is worried about my safety,' explained Cordelia. 'Especially after the death of Miss Crane.'

'A laudable concern,' said Padlow, having recovered his composure. 'But I can assure you I will make every effort to try to protect her.'

'Have you got a gun?' Luke asked Cordelia.

'Ladies don't carry guns,' said a shocked Padlow.

'I've got a small gun. It only holds one bullet. But it fits in my handbag.'

'Right. See that it's cleaned and oiled. Whenever you go out I want you to carry it with you.'

'I think that all this talk about guns is unseemly,' protested Padlow.

'Right. I'm on my way.' Luke

addressed Cordelia.

Cordelia went towards him. She kissed him on the lips. 'Take care, Luke,' she whispered, as he went out through the door.

'And so is kissing a married man like that,' added a shocked Padlow.

19

Luke had been riding at an easy pace for a couple of hours before deciding that it was time to take a rest. He was riding on the prairie with only a few cottonwood trees dotted here and there to break up the landscape. He reined his horse to a halt and, as a result of years of practice as a lawman, he instinctively glanced behind him. He received a shock which jolted him to complete awareness. There were two riders following him.

He was convinced that they were following him by the speed with which they disappeared behind a convenient tree when he had pulled up. He hesitated for a moment while he decided his next move. They were about a quarter of a mile away and would probably be wondering whether he had spotted them when he had turned in the saddle.

They were too far away and their movements had been too quick for him to identify them. He felt reasonably secure, since they were obviously not going to come too close until it was safe for them to do so. The advantage lay with him also in the fact that they couldn't be completely sure whether he had spotted them or not. The best course of action for him therefore was to confuse them further by taking the rest he had intended taking — all the time keeping a wary eye on them.

He gave his horse water, then, after eating the bread and cheese his landlady had supplied him with and taking a drink from his canteen, he set out again. He deliberately kept his horse galloping at a steady pace without increasing its speed. This helped to conserve its energy should it be required later.

Who were they? The question kept hammering at him as he rode along. The trail he was following which led from Crossville to Herford was deserted at this time in the morning. Indeed it was usually deserted for most of the day, its only regular travellers being aboard the stage, which used the trail a couple of times a week — but not today, Luke concluded. However his thoughts about the stage led to the stage hold-up. In fact he was probably riding along the part of the trail where the hold-up had taken place. Did the fact that he was being followed by the two riders have anything to do with the fact that five men had held up the stage? Were these two members of Mellor's gang? Were they in fact the two that he and poor Daisy had spotted in Crossville?

Luke kept a wary eye on them by turning quickly every time he stopped for a drink. They seemed to be keeping the same distance behind him, which could suggest that they were biding their time until they found a suitable spot to spring an attack on him. They would know, of course, that he would reach Herford some time late in the day, if he kept riding at this pace. So presumably they would have to make their move in the afternoon.

It was in fact the middle of the afternoon when Luke had an opportunity to find out who they were. So far, after about five hours of riding, he hadn't met a soul. There were no cattle grazing on the inhospitable mixture of sand and tufted grass which made up the prairie. His only constant companions were the vultures which wheeled overhead. You won't be getting me for your next meal, he promised them. However when he spotted a group of riders heading towards him, he realized that the scene could be about to change.

He fished in his shirt-pocket. He produced something which he hadn't found any use for in over a year. It was his old marshal's badge. For some reason which he couldn't quite recollect he had never given his badge in after he had stepped down from the position of marshal of Crossville. Now the badge could come in useful. He pinned it to his shirt.

The riders approached. He counted six. That made his plan perfect. If there had only been, say, three then the odds against its success would have been less favourable. As they approached him he reined in his horse. He guessed that the two following him would have noted that he had pulled up and would have done the same.

The riders were now near enough for Luke to see that they were cowboys. He guessed that they were cowboys who were coming to Crossville to find the seasonal work there at round-up time. They stopped when they reached him.

'Howdy, Marshal,' said the leader.

'I want you to do me a favour,' said Luke. 'In the first place I want you to form a circle round me. Don't ask me why — just do it.'

The note of authority in Luke's voice made them do as he asked without demur. When he was satisfied that they were in position he outlined the next part of his plan.

Clinker and Pedro, the two riders who had been following Luke, regarded the group of riders without any obvious concern.

'Maybe Tilling is asking them the way to Herford,' suggested Pedro.

Clinker laughed.

They watched while the cowboys started to ride towards them. Tilling, it seemed, was now behind them and had restarted on his way to Herford. The six cowboys drew nearer.

'Don't say anything to them,' warned Pedro.

'Why not?' asked a puzzled Clinker.

'We don't want them to remember us, do we? Mellor told us to try not to get recognized.'

'Oh, I see,' said Clinker.

When the cowboys were about a hundred yards away a strange thing happened. One of them broke ranks and started racing towards them. An even stranger thing happened when he started firing at them.

Too late they realized that the person they had assumed was a cowboy, was in fact Tilling. He fired two shots at Pedro, killing him instantly. Clinker was still struggling to draw his revolver when Luke emptied the rest of his bullets into him.

'That was good shooting, Marshal,' said the leader of the cowboys.

'Help me to bury them,' said Luke. Any reluctance on the part of the cowboys was dispelled when Luke produced a ten-dollar note.

'There's one of these each for you for helping to catch a couple of dangerous outlaws,' he stated.

20

Luke rode into Herford late in the evening. He stopped at a saloon that advertised rooms to let. He booked a room.

'Can I get you something to drink?' demanded the buxom landlady.

'No, but I'll have a meal.'

'Will steak be all right?'

'Steak will be fine.'

After an excellent meal Luke ordered a bath. While the landlady was filling the tub, Luke asked: 'Is Tom Milton still the sheriff here?'

'Yes, he's been here now for several years. He always talks about retiring, but they'll have to drag him out of the office before he retires.'

The following morning, after breakfast, Luke strolled down Main Street towards the sheriff's office. Herford was a bustling town which had become even busier since the arrival of the railroad a few months earlier.

The sheriff greeted Luke warmly.

'It's great to see you again. I know it's early in the morning, but can I offer you a drink, Luke?'

'No, thanks, Tom. I'm on the wagon. I drank too much after our daughter died and so I'm now off the stuff.'

'Very wise, too. I'm still drinking Dan's whiskey and my wife is convinced that it's rotting my stomach. Now what can I do for you, Luke?'

'I killed two men on the way here. They were members of an outlaw gang led by a guy called Mellor.' He described how the two had been following him and how he had managed to turn the tables on them with the help of some cowboys.

'That was a smart move,' said the sheriff, appreciatively. 'Do you know the names of these outlaws?'

'Clinker and Pedro. They're buried out there on the prairie. But I've brought their guns and gunbelts in.

Their names are on their holsters.'

The sheriff examined the belts.

'I think we can accept them as evidence.'

'If you want more confirmation I'm sure I can find the cowboys when I return to Crossville. They'll be working on some ranch or other.'

'No, these belts will be enough. There's one thing though that maybe you haven't thought about.'

'What's that?'

'Now that you are no longer a lawman, you can claim bounty on those two. Especially if they're in our rogues' gallery.'

'I know where they are.' The deputy, Frank Gardner, who had so far not contributed to the conversation, chipped in.

He led Luke to a group of drawings on the far end of the wall. Luke studied them interestedly. 'So these are five of the Mellor gang. Well, three now,' he corrected himself.

'As you can see there's five hundred

dollars reward on Mellor and three hundred for each of the gang,' said the deputy.

'You've already earned yourself six hundred dollars by getting rid of two of the outlaws,' said the sheriff. 'It's not bad for a day's work.'

Luke was still studying them. 'Mellor I will recognize anywhere,' he stated. 'I want to make sure that I recognize North and Hitchings when I see them.'

'Weren't the pictures in the office in Crossville?' asked the deputy.

'No. I asked about them, but the marshal, Summers, said he hadn't got them,' said Luke.

'That's strange,' said the deputy. 'We've had these since' — he examined the date on one of the drawings — 'since last November. Six months.'

'All the drawings would have gone round to all the law offices, as you know, Luke,' said the sheriff.

'Yes, that is strange,' said Luke reflectively.

He accepted the sheriff's offer to go

to the bank to collect the bounty money. He was accompanied by the deputy.

'We've got three banks now in Herford,' said the deputy, proudly.

'Yes, it's a booming town,' Luke agreed. 'When Tom retires you'll step into a nice job.'

'Can you ever see Tom retiring?'

'No, I suppose not,' replied Luke, with a chuckle. 'He's one of those lawmen who'll go on for ever.'

'Are you ever thinking of taking it up again?'

'Maybe. But I've got some business to settle first.'

At the bank Luke received his six hundred dollars.

'You can open an account here and deposit the money,' suggested the bank-manager.

'Right,' said Luke. 'I'll deposit five hundred and keep a hundred.'

'A wise move,' replied the bank-manager. 'Especially with all these criminals around — no reflection on the excellent work you're doing, Deputy,' he added, hastily.

'Well at least there'll be two less now,' replied the deputy, 'Thanks to Luke.'

Luke, who was not used to being praised, reddened.

'I'll be on my way,' he told the deputy. 'I've got a train to catch.'

'Good luck,' said the deputy.

I've certainly been lucky so far, reflected Luke. The question is — will it continue.

21

Luke reached Chicago later that evening. He still couldn't get over the marvel of train travel which could transport a person from one place to another so much more speedily than going by horse. Normally he would have looked for a boarding-house which had a room vacant, but he remembered that he was a hundred dollars richer than he had expected so he chose a hotel for the night. It turned out, though, that the meal wasn't half as good as the one he had had in Herford. Even the bath which the pretty maid filled for him was less than satisfactory with its tepid water. So much for choosing to mix with the wealthy, he concluded, as he prepared to hit the hay.

In the morning he set out for an address in Maddox Street. After receiving a couple of wrong directions from pedestrians he eventually found it. It was in a row of terraced grey houses. He knocked with the knocker. A familiar figure opened the door. She was an attractive woman in her late twenties.

'Hullo, Ruth,' said Luke.

'I've been expecting you for the past few weeks. You'd better come in.'

He was led into a small, tastefully furnished sitting-room. They sat down facing each other. For a while neither spoke as they stared at each other. At last Luke said: 'You're looking well, Ruth.'

'You're looking . . . better than I expected.'

'I'm on the wagon. I haven't been drinking for a couple of weeks.'

'That's great. I hope that you don't think it affects our relationship, though.'

'No. As you said in your last letter — it's over. That's why I'm here.'

Ruth was still staring at him. 'So what do you do now?'

'I've become a bounty hunter. It's quite well paid.'

'I'll get you some coffee.'

When she returned with the coffees, Luke had lit a cigar.

'I didn't know you smoked cigars.'

'I usually don't. Partly because I can't afford it. But I've come into some money so I decided to give myself a treat.'

'You've got some money as a bounty hunter?'

'That's right.' Luke described how he had tricked Clinker and Pedro and had ended up by killing them.

'How much did you get?'

'Six hundred dollars.'

'Six hundred? But that's almost as much as you used to get in a year when you were a marshal.'

'I know.'

'To think that we scrimped and saved on the poor pay you used to get as a marshal.'

'I could have taken bribes. But I never would.'

'No, you were too honest for your own good. And where did it get you?'

'There's no point in arguing. It's all water under the bridge.'

'We had some good times.' She was regarding him with a fixed stare.

'You mean before the accident.'

'Yes. We were always good in bed together.'

'Yes, we were.'

They were staring at each other as though trying to read each other's minds.

'There hasn't been anybody else since I came here. You believe that, don't you?'

'Yes.'

'I've got a suggestion to make.' She came to sit on the arm of his chair.

'What suggestion?'

'I own the house now. My aunt's will has finally been settled. I've got the house and a couple of hundred dollars a year. It's enough for me to live on.'

'It was generous of her to leave some of her money to you.'

She leaned over and started running her hands though his hair. It reminded him of time gone by. Some of their love-making would start this way. Then she would move on to his lap. And things would take their natural turn from there. As Ruth said, they had always been good together in bed.

'The money doesn't all have to be mine.' A husky tone had come into her voice.

'What are you suggesting?'

'Oh, come off it, Luke. Don't pretend you're slow on the uptake. You've given up drinking. You haven't any ties in Crossville. You could move in here. The bed is big enough for both of us,' she ended, suggestively.

'You mean we could make a fresh start?'

'You've got it. You're not so stupid after all.'

She slid on to his lap. Somehow her lips found his. At first his response was cool. But gradually the familiar touch of her lips, her hair brushing against his cheek revived feelings which had lain dormant for over a year.

'Mm,' she said, contentedly, as she adjusted her body to a more comfortable position.

'Let's get this straight. The fact that we've had one kiss doesn't mean that I've agreed to your suggestion.'

'Of course not, dear,' she said, guiding his mouth to hers again.

When they broke apart she said: 'I'm still not thirty. We could think about having another child. I know it would never be the same — Annabelle could never be replaced — but we could make a fresh start. This town would be ideal for you. They're always advertising for lawmen in Pinkertons. What do you say?'

She held him at arm's length while she examined his face.

'I don't know. I've got some business to finish off in Crossville.'

She twisted her face into a scowl of displeasure.

'What business could you possibly

have to finish in Crossville? Apart from paying your landlady the rent. You could always send that on to her by mail.'

'I've got three more outlaws to catch.'

'What's catching more outlaws got to do with you? You've killed two of them — leave it at that. Next time you might be the one who gets killed.'

'One of them is the one I saw when I was with Annabelle. If you remember we went for our guns. That's when I let go of Annabelle's hand and she ran in front of the horse.'

She jumped off his lap. 'If you're going on this revenge trail, then I take back what I said about us starting together again.'

'It's something I've got to do,' he said, stubbornly.

'Annabelle is dead, don't you understand? It broke my heart when she died, just as it broke yours. But we've got to move on.' She kneeled in front of him and took his hands. 'You've given up drinking. It shows that you've almost got over it. Don't go back to Crossville. Stay here with me. We can be happy together again. We can make a fresh start. Not many people get the chance that we're getting.'

He got to his feet and pulled her up gently.

'This idea of us starting back together is all a bit sudden. You've got to give me time.'

'How much time do you want?' she demanded bitterly. 'You've already had more than a year. I can't wait for ever.'

'There's range war brewing in Crossville. I've got to see a lawyer here and he should be able to give me the information I need to stop the war.'

'What's it got to do with you?' Her voice was raised in exasperation.

'It's just something I've got to do,' he responded, stubbornly.

'All right. This is what we'll do.' She calmed down as she went to a writing-desk in the corner of the room. She produced an official document. 'The lawyer said your signature on this will be enough for me to start divorce proceedings. If you sign it now I'll keep it here for a week. That will give you enough time to sort things out in Crossville. If you're not back in a week's time I'll take this to the lawyer and he'll start the divorce proceedings. But if you come back before the week's over, I'll tear it up.'

He stared at her. This was a more determined Ruth than he remembered. Cordelia had called her weak, but in the year's absence she had seemed to have found a new strength.

'Is that a deal?'

'That's a deal.'

She held out her hand and they shook formally.

'Right. You'd better go and see your lawyer. Your week will soon be up.'

22

The Red Garter saloon was busy. The pianist had been hitting the piano keyboard with the kind of enthusiasm he reserved for busy nights. The singer, who with her make-up would have passed for eighteen but without it would have looked at least ten years older, was happily regarding the spittoon which on music nights would hold her takings. Already she guessed there were several dollars in it. And there would be more by the end of the night if the cowboys kept tossing coins into it as they had been during the past hour or so.

She glanced at the pianist, who was finishing his drink, happy in the knowledge that another free one would appear at his elbow.

'We'll give them Dixie,' said the singer, whose name was Paula. It was a song that was always guaranteed to keep the drinkers in a good mood, even though it had been the song of the Confederates in the Civil War. Fortunately hardly any in the bar could remember the war and so they accepted the song as a rousing tune.

> 'Oh, I wish I was in the land of cotton,
> Old times there are not forgotten,
> Look away, look away, look away Dixie land.

Many of them joined in the chorus.

> I wish I was in Dixie, Hooray! Hooray!
> In Dixie land I'll take my stand
> To live and die in Dixie.
> Away! Away! Away down south in Dixie.

The singer was right. The audience wanted a second chorus. When at last she went to the bar to get some refreshments she was greeted by a cowboy.

'That was a lovely song, ma'am. Can I get you a drink?'

She was used to having her drinks bought for her.

'Thank you. I'll have a whiskey and lemonade.'

While they were waiting for the drinks to appear she said, conversationally:

'I haven't seen you here before, have I?'

'No, ma'am. We only came into town yesterday.'

'We?'

'Me and my five friends. Actually we had a bit of luck.'

'You've won some money at cards?'

'No. We helped to kill a couple of outlaws.'

'How could it be lucky to kill a couple of outlaws?' She was intrigued.

He described how they met Luke on the prairie and how he had tricked the two outlaws and shot them.

'He gave us ten dollars each for helping him.'

'I think he should have given you more. He'll probably get a few hundred in bounty money for killing the outlaws.'

'I think you're wrong, ma'am. Actually he was a lawman. If I understand it right, then a lawman can't claim bounty money.'

'I think you're right there, cowboy. Well, if you'll excuse me, I'll get back to my singing. Thanks for the drink.'

'My pleasure, ma'am.'

Although the bar was crowded there was a bystander who managed to overhear the conversation. When the singer returned to the rostrum he went in search of his friend. He found him watching a game of cards. He managed to attract his attention.

'Listen, North, I've just found out something important.'

North reluctantly turned his attention from watching the card-players.

'Tilling has killed Clinker and Pedro.'

The singer was starting her next

song. 'The yellow rose of Texas', and any conversation was forbidden while she was singing. The person whom Hitchings had been addressing, North, was forced to wait until the end of the song to find out what his companion had been trying to reveal.

When Hitchings eventually gave him the details of the conversation he had overheard at the bar, North shook his head in disbelief.

'They are both dead?'

'That's what the cowboy over by the bar said. He said that Tilling had killed them. Apparently he had pretended to be a lawman. By doing that he had tricked them and shot them.'

'So that's why they didn't return to the camp yesterday.'

'I would say that's obvious,' Hitchings snapped.

'All right, there's no need to get sore with me. You know what we've got to do now?'

'Go back to the camp and tell the boss.'

'And you know what he'll say?'

'The same as he told Clinker and Pedro. Get Tilling.'

'At all costs.'

'I don't know about you, but I need another drink before going to the camp and facing the boss.'

'I agree. I think we'd better take an extra bottle of whiskey back for him, too.'

23

When Luke eventually returned to Crossville the evening was drawing in. He had one predominant thought in his mind — namely that he needed a good night's rest after his journey back from Chicago.

He had left his horse in the livery stable and when he approached the church house he could see the lamp which had been lit in the parlour. He could also see a figure sitting in the porch. Could it be Cordelia?

On closer inspection it proved to be her father. He was sitting in the porch smoking his pipe.

'Hullo, Luke. I'm just enjoying my last pipe of the day. I suppose you wouldn't care to join me?'

Luke would have liked to have gone on his way, but he felt he could hardly refuse the invitation. He sat down on the bench.

The preacher offered him his pouch of tobacco, but Luke refused politely and produced his cigars.

'I didn't know you smoked cigars.' Where had he heard that remark before? Oh, yes, from Ruth.

'I don't usually. But I've come into some money, and I'm having a treat.'

'I'm too polite to ask you how you came into the money — although I'm dying to know.'

Luke smiled. He told the preacher about his encounter with the two outlaws, and how, as a result he was entitled to the bounty money.

'That's good news for you. I'm sure when I tell Cordelia that it will lift her spirits.'

Luke caught the implication. 'She's not ill, is she?'

'Not exactly. She's just got a heavy cold. The doctor told her to stay indoors for a couple of days.'

Luke stood up to leave. 'I'll call to see her tomorrow. I've got some other news for her.'

'I'd better tell you my news before you go. The quarrel between the homesteaders and Mr Oliver has escalated. One of Mr Oliver's cowboys rode through one of the homesteader's farms. The homesteader shot at him. He said he was just trying to scare him off. Sadly, the bullet hit the cowboy.'

'What happened?' demanded Luke, although he felt he already knew the answer.

'The cowboy was killed,' stated the preacher.

* * *

The following morning Luke awoke early. His landlady, Mrs Blinkley, was usually up before him and in the kitchen, raking out the fire before he had risen. But this morning he had stoked up the fire and was boiling the kettle to make his coffee when she descended the stairs.

'My, we are up early this morning,' she said.

'I've got an urgent call to make,' replied Luke.

'Yes, I did hear the preacher's daughter was ill.'

'I'm not talking about going there. I'm going to see Wilbur Daniels.'

'You've heard about the war between the homesteaders and Mr Oliver then?'

'Is that what they're calling it?' demanded a horrified Luke.

'What else can it be? One of the homesteaders shot one of Mr Oliver's cowboys and killed him. You don't think Oliver would take that lying down?'

'No, I don't suppose he would.' Luke finished his coffee.

'Aren't you going to have breakfast?' she enquired, as he put on his jacket.

'I'm sorry, I haven't got time,' said Luke. 'With luck I might be able to prevent some more killings.'

A few minutes later he was hurrying down Main Street. He glanced across at the church house as he passed it. He would have liked to have a leisurely morning and to call in to see whether

Cordelia had recovered from her cold, but he knew that his present errand was more important.

The owner of the livery stable voiced the same remark as Luke's landlady.

'You're up and about early. I doubt whether your horse has finished his oats yet.'

'Well tell him to get a move on. I'm in a hurry.'

It was the kind of comment that the owner of the livery stable received regularly. It was usually delivered in a half-serious manner by the person waiting for his horse. But not by Luke this morning. His face was set in hard lines which deterred the other from making any comment of his own.

Five minutes later Luke was galloping up Main Street as though he were racing in the Kentucky Derby.

24

When Luke arrived in Wilbur's farm its owner was collecting some eggs from the hen house that stood near the corner of the house. However it was not Wilbur's hens that held Luke's attention, but the shocking sight which had transformed Wilbur's front door. He had nailed about a dozen Indian scalps to it.

'I learned how to take scalps when I was fighting the Indians,' said Wilbur, proudly. 'You cut them from the centre of the forehead. It's quite easy.'

Luke jumped down from his horse.

'I came here to try to get things sorted out between the homesteaders and Oliver and all you're doing is aggravating the situation,' snapped Luke.

'There's no need to get ornery about it,' replied Wilbur. 'I was going to offer you some eggs, but I don't think I will bother now.'

'Suit yourself. But before I go you'd better hear what I found out from the lawyer in Chicago.'

'If you've got some news, you'd better come in,' said Wilbur, ungraciously.

When they were seated in the living-room, Luke began.

'I went to see Mr Chiddlehurst in Chicago. He's a lawyer I had some dealings with when I was town marshal.'

'What did he say?'

'He said it all depended whether you received notice that you should pay your taxes during the past seven years. If you've received those notices and refused to pay your taxes then legally they can force you to pay them now. On the other hand, if you didn't receive any notices during those seven years then the town council can't claim any back payment from you.'

Wilbur's face lit up. 'Is that a fact?'

'I got the lawyer to write it all down.'

'I never received any demands for taxes during the seven years I've been here. I'm sure the other homesteaders are in the same position.'

'So you can stop this nonsense about fighting Oliver. And for a start you can take those horrible things off your door.'

'So we don't have to pay the back taxes.' Wilbur repeated, as if to try to convince himself of the truth of Luke's statement.

'That's right. Now you can fry me a couple of those eggs. I didn't have time for breakfast.'

After Wilbur had fried the eggs and he and Luke were drinking their coffees, Luke described how he had killed the outlaws who had been following him on the way to Heford.

'That was a good trick,' said Wilbur, appreciatively. 'But you'd better be careful. The other outlaws are going to go all out to get you.'

'I know. But at least there are only

three of them left now.'

They finished their cigarettes. As Luke stood up to leave Wilbur said: 'Thanks for finding out about whether we should pay our taxes.'

'It was either that or watching you foolhardy bunch of homesteaders get involved in a war with Oliver.'

'I'll go and tell the other homesteaders the good news,' said Wilbur, as Luke walked to his horse.

'And take those disgusting things down and burn them,' said Luke, sternly.

He started to ride slowly back to Crossville in a happier frame of mind than when he had ridden out. True, there was the business of the homesteader who had shot one of Oliver's cowboys to be resolved. But it really wasn't any of his business. He wasn't the town marshal any longer. It was up to Summers to bring the homesteader to face trial. Then it would be up to a jury to decide whether the killing had been justified.

No, that wasn't anything to do with him now, but there remained the unfinished business between himself and Mellor. That still had to be resolved one way or the other. As Wilbur had said, he'd better be careful. Well, that was just what he intended to be from now on.

His reverie was interrupted by the sound of a shot. It came from behind him. He reckoned it was a rifle shot which came from a distance of about a mile or so away. A terrible fear gripped him. Could it have come from Wilbur's house?

He swung his horse around and spurred it savagely to get back to the farm. As he approached, at first sight everything appeared normal. Wilbur's horse was grazing in the paddock. There was no sign of Wilbur, or of any other human being. Perhaps he had been mistaken. The sounds of gunfire are notoriously deceptive. Sometimes it was difficult to gauge from which direction they came, let alone how far away they were.

Some of the hens scattered as he rode towards the front of the house. Suddenly he spotted what he had been dreading to see. A body was slumped near the front door. It was Wilbur's.

He leapt from his horse. Wilbur was lying facing the door and there was an ominous red stain on his back. Luke knelt by his side. At first he thought he was already dead, but Wilbur managed to half-open his eyes.

'What a way to finish up,' he gasped.

'Don't talk, I'll get you to the doctor's,' said Luke, gently.

'It's too late. I've seen enough dead bodies to know when it's too late. There's one thing you can do for me though.' He went into a fit of coughing. Blood was already coming from his mouth. Luke knew in his heart that it was indeed too late.

'I managed to catch a glimpse of him. He had a scar down the side of his cheek. I want you to promise to get him.'

'I promise.'

For a moment an almost contented smile flitted across Wilbur's face. Then his eyes glazed over. Luke, who had been controlling his own emotion until then, could contain it no more.

He stood up. 'You bastard!' he shouted in the direction he assumed the horseman would have taken to escape.

25

The early-morning shoppers in Crossville were witnesses to a strange sight. A wagon was being driven down Main Street. This in itself was not unusual. Many kinds of horse-drawn transport were driven down Main Street, from buggies to stagecoaches. What was unusual about the wagon was that it obviously held a body which had been wrapped in a blanket.

The face of the man driving the wagon was set in hard lines. Indeed some of the shoppers had to look twice to convince themselves that it was indeed their ex-lawman. None of them had ever seen such an expression on Luke's face, which looked as though it had been carved out of stone.

He drew up outside the doctor's house. In answer to Luke's knock a maid answered the door.

'Is Doctor Gribble in?'

'He's just having his breakfast.'

'Tell him this is urgent.'

Luke's tone was sufficient for her to go scuttling back into the house.

The doctor, who prided himself that he had seen every kind of sickness and human mortality, was nevertheless shocked when he viewed the effect of the rifle shot on Wilbur's back.

'Bring him into the spare room,' he commanded Luke.

Luke carried the corpse into the room and deposited it on the long table which the doctor reserved for his operations.

'I can get the bullet out,' he told Luke. 'But I don't think it will prove anything.'

'It came from a .22 rifle,' stated Luke.

'How do you know?' The doctor glanced at him with interest.

'I heard the shot. It was obviously a rifle. When I arrived at Wilbur's farm he was just dying.'

Luke repeated the same statement to the marshal when he arrived at the doctor's house about ten minutes later.

'What were you doing at Wilbur's farm that early in the morning?' demanded Summers.

'I had some news for him. I went to tell him that he didn't have to pay the back taxes that the council were charging the homesteaders. In fact none of them would have to pay. It was an illegal charge.'

'How did you work that out?' snapped Summers.

'I went to see a lawyer in Chicago. Somebody I could trust. He explained that the homesteaders could only be forced to pay if they had received demands to pay during the past seven years and had refused to pay. None of them had received any demands.'

'That certainly sounds reasonable,' said the doctor.

'That's nothing to do with me,' snapped Summers. 'That's the business of another department.'

'Wilbur was going out to tell the other homesteaders the good news when he was shot,' said Luke, bitterly.

'What's going to happen now?' the doctor asked Luke, not Summers.

'My guess is it will blow up into a full homesteaders' war. One of Oliver's cowboys has been killed — now one of the homesteaders. It only takes a spark to start such a conflict off. And this one has been festering for several years.'

Luke noticed that Summers had paled at the suggestion of a war between Oliver and the homesteaders.

'Shouldn't you swear in more deputies?' The doctor addressed the remark to Summers.

'It's only Tilling's opinion that this thing will escalate,' stated Summers.

'How many more killings do you want before you do something about it?' Luke was shouting. 'There have already been four in the past three weeks. That's more than I had during the whole time I was the town marshal.'

'Yes, the difference is that now I'm

the town marshal and I do things my way,' snapped Summers. He turned on his heel and stormed out of the house.

'You didn't get much co-operation from him there, did you?' stated the doctor, drily.

'I wonder why,' said Luke, thoughtfully.

'You think he might be in league with Oliver in order to keep this homesteaders' war going?'

'It's a possibility. Every time I mention taking on extra deputies he turns down the suggestion.'

'Of course, if he is in Oliver's pay it won't be the first time that a rich rancher has had a lawman in his pocket. Oh, I'm not suggesting that when you were a lawman — '

'It's all right. My wife accused me of being too honest.'

'Your wife? You're not divorced then?'

'Not yet.'

'I'm sorry. I didn't mean to pry. Somehow I assumed . . . '

'Yes — well, all that's in the past.'

Luke turned to leave.

'I'm afraid I've got more bad news for you,' said the doctor.

'I'm afraid I've had all the bad news I can stand this morning. Still suppose I'd better hear it.'

'It's about Cordelia.'

'Her father told me she had a heavy cold.'

'I'm afraid it's worse than that. She's got tuberculosis. I've suspected it for some time. Yesterday she started coughing up blood.'

26

It took a big effort on Luke's part to visit Cordelia that same afternoon. It took an even bigger effort to pretend that she was not seriously ill.

She was lying in bed with her hair spread loosely over the pillow. 'I'm sorry I can't get up to greet you, Luke. The doctor says I must stay in bed for a few days.'

Luke choked. He couldn't trust himself to speak. He tried to hide his confusion by holding out the flowers he had brought.

'Beautiful flowers for a beautiful lady.'

She smiled. 'It's almost worth not seeing you for a few days just to receive one of your compliments.'

He put the flowers on the dressing-table. Cordelia patted the side of the bed, indicating he should sit there.

'So what have you been up to these past few days? By the way, I know about your success in killing two of the outlaws — Daddy told me. It was a very clever move.'

Luke told her about his visit to Chicago, missing out the fact that he had visited Ruth.

'So the homesteaders were right in refusing to pay their taxes?'

'Yes, they were quite right. Unfortunately it was too late for one of them.'

'Yes, I heard about Wilbur Daniels. You were there?'

He described his visit and how he had returned to find Wilbur dying. Cordelia grasped his hand. Was it his imagination or was her own hand thinner than it used to be.

'Do you think that Oliver hired the outlaws?'

'I think so. He's the only one who's got something to gain by starting a homesteaders' war.'

'And you think that this outlaw, Mellor, was behind the killing of Miss Crane?'

'Ah, that's where we hit a snag.'

'In what way?' She moved her head on the pillow to make herself more comfortable.

'Why should the outlaw, Mellor, call to see her?'

'Because she would be able to identify a couple of his gang.'

'She had already done that. We saw them coming out of the saloon.'

'Yes, but Mellor wouldn't know that, would he?'

'Of course there is another explanation.'

'Which is?'

'That he came to see somebody in the town and told him about Miss Crane. Then that person killed her.'

She shivered. 'You've always thought that Miss Crane invited her killer into the house, haven't you? You've always had a suspicion that it was Summers.'

'It certainly points that way, since there were two coffee-cups there. And there's one other thing.'

'What's that?'

'When Summers came into Miss Crane's house he went straight through the living-room into the kitchen. A person's normal reaction would have been to ask where the body was. It could just as easily have been upstairs in the bedroom. But he went into the kitchen because he knew the body was there. He had killed her.'

This time she shivered uncontrollably. Luke put his arms around her. He brushed her hair tenderly. The maid knocked and entered. She seemed surprised to see Cordelia in Luke's arms.

'I'm just going,' Luke announced. 'I'll be back later.'

'Take care,' Cordelia whispered.

Luke left the house and walked slowly along the street. Why was everything going wrong all at the same time? First Wilbur getting shot. Now Cordelia dying of tuberculosis. He had no doubt that she was going to die. He had felt how thin she had become when he was holding her. When she had been wearing her clothes normally he hadn't noticed that she had become thinner. But ten minutes ago it had become obvious.

His footsteps led him to the café as if by their own volition. He automatically sat at the corner table which he had often occupied with Cordelia. Would she ever again sit opposite him here? A terrible anger shook him at the injustice of it all. He wanted to shout out against it as he had shouted against the injustice of Wilbur getting killed.

'Do you mind if I sit here?'

He hadn't taken any notice of the comings and goings in the café. He glanced up. It was Stephen, Daisy Crane's brother. Luke didn't reply, but indicated the empty chair with his hand.

Stephen ordered his coffee. He could see that Luke wasn't in the mood for conversation.

He kept glancing at Luke. At last he said: 'I've got some news for you.'

'That's your job, isn't it? Reporting

news,' said Luke, coldly.

Stephen sighed. He knew this wasn't going to be easy, but for some reason which he couldn't fathom it was more difficult than he thought it would be.

'It's about the homesteaders.'

'I know all about the homesteaders. One of my friends was a homesteader. He was murdered this morning.'

'I know. I'm sorry. Do you know that the other homesteaders are planning their revenge?'

Luke plucked up interest. 'What are they going to do?'

'They're going to attack Oliver's ranch.'

'Oh, my God!' This time the exclamation was loud enough for some of the other customers to glance at Luke.

'I came back from seeing a few of them a couple of hours ago. I wanted a story for my newspaper. They said they were getting their guns ready. One of them said that if it was the last thing he did he was going to avenge Wilbur's death.'

Luke's hand automatically went to his own gun. The gesture was not lost on Stephen.

Luke stood up. 'If you stay here you might have a better story at the end of the day.'

'I'm not staying. If you're going out to help the homesteaders, I'm coming with you.'

Luke stared at him. 'It's not your fight.'

'It's not yours either. Anyhow it's as much mine as yours. My sister was killed by one of those outlaws. According to the homesteaders the three who are left are helping Oliver.'

'You're not going to be much use unless you can handle a gun.'

'I was training to be a cavalryman. I was in the army for nine months. They taught me how to shoot.'

'Come on then.'

They hurried out of the café.

'They didn't even finish their coffees,' observed the lady at the next table.

27

The two horsemen were riding like the wind towards Oliver's ranch. *Would they be in time to prevent bloodshed?* The thought pounded in Luke's head to the rhythm of the horse's hoofs.

They hadn't spoken since they left the café. When they had come to the livery stable, Luke had noted with approval that Stephen had thumbed bullets into his revolver. Maybe he would have a chance to avenge his sister's death. Maybe, too, he, Luke, would have a chance to avenge Wilbur's killing.

Wilbur had stated that the guy who had shot him had had a scar down his cheek. That fitted the picture of one of the outlaws he had seen in Herford when he had visited the sheriff there. The outlaw's name was North. He couldn't wait to catch up with him. He spurred his horse to even greater effort.

The answer whether they would be too late to prevent bloodshed came when they could both hear the sounds of distant guns. They were still a couple of miles away from the ranch, but there was no mistaking the sounds of the rifles.

They were riding between low hills and the ranch was still hidden in the distance. Suddenly they both saw it. A red glow in the sky.

'Is that the northern lights?' demanded Stephen.

'It's Oliver's ranch. It's on fire,' replied Luke, grimly.

When they were nearer they could see the full effect of the fire. During the years when Luke had ridden out to the ranch he had often been puzzled as to why such a prosperous farmer as Oliver would live in a wooden ranch. True, most of the buildings in Crossville were wooden structures, but the original ranch-owner should have been rich enough to build a stone structure that would have been largely safe from fire. Whatever the reason for putting up a wooden building, the tragedy of such a choice was now obvious.

'The homesteaders are firing from behind the wall,' shouted Stephen.

There was a low wall beyond the gate that led to the house. When the smoke parted Luke could see the tell-tale flashes from their guns. It was obvious that there were gunmen inside the house firing at the homesteaders. The question was how much longer were they going to be able to stay in the burning building.

Apart from the noise of the guns and the crackling of the flames another sound contributed to the clamour — the horses in the coral were going wild with terror. Some of them were charging at the fences, trying to escape from the smoke which already covered the corral and from the flames which were getting nearer. The pitiful screams of some of the foals contributed to the din.

As Luke and Stephen rode towards the blazing structure they could see that parts of the roof were already falling away. Engulfed in flames one large section of it fell to the ground. Surely the gunmen inside couldn't stay there much longer? Suddenly, as if in answer to Luke's assumption a figure ran out of the building. To Luke's surprise it wasn't one of the gunmen but Oliver himself. As if by some unspecified agreement the homesteaders behind the wall stopped firing. Luke could see through the swirling smoke that Oliver was carrying something in his arms. His surprise at seeing the ranch-owner running out in the open space between the two sets of guns changed to amazement when he saw what Oliver was carrying. He was carrying a pile of books! He placed them on the ground. For a moment a cloud of smoke obscured the rancher and left Luke wondering whether he had imagined the whole scene. Then the smoke cleared and the rancher could be seen scurrying back into the house — presumably to fetch more of his precious books.

Suddenly three gunmen burst out of the house. In the swirling smoke Luke couldn't see their faces clearly. His guess was that they were Mellor and his two henchmen. They ran out into the open space which had just been occupied by Oliver. For a moment they were concentrating on the homesteaders in front of them who had started firing again. Luke and Stephen were now near enough to take part in the battle.

'Mellor,' shouted Luke.

One of the gunmen swung round to fire at him. He was too late. Luke shot him in the chest. For good measure he pumped another couple of bullets into him.

Stephen had followed Luke's example. His first bullet hit one of the remaining outlaws in the face. He emptied the rest of his bullets into him as he staggered and finally fell.

The third outlaw threw away his revolver and raised his hands in the universally recognized gesture of surrender.

'Don't shoot,' cried Luke. 'It's all over.'

Then the unexpected happened, as it often does in gunfights. Oliver came out of the house, once more carrying an armful of books. Obviously one of the homesteaders hadn't heard Luke's cry. He fired at Oliver. By some fluke, since none of the homesteaders had hit any of their other intended targets, this bullet hit Oliver. He dropped down dead.

⋆ ⋆ ⋆

Later Luke reported the results of the homesteaders' war, as it became to be called, to Cordelia.

'So Mellor is dead, and one of the outlaws?'

'Yes, Stephen shot him. I was quite impressed.'

'He acted out of revenge. The same as you.'

'I suppose so.'

'What about Oliver? He behaved strangely, didn't he?'

'Very much so. In fact I've changed my mind about Oliver.'

'What do you mean?'

'Remember I said that I suspected that Stephen's sister had been killed by someone she knew — or at least someone she trusted.'

'That's why she made him a cup of coffee?'

'Exactly. Well I think that person was Oliver. He called to see her and killed her so that he could go ahead with his plan to take over the homesteaders' farms.'

'It seems a bit far-fetched.'

'Of course I'd never be able to prove it now. But one other thing points to it — he slit Daisy's throat. As a farmer he would have killed dozens of his livestock that way.'

'Also no person in their right senses

would have run out into the middle of a gunfight to try to save his books.'

'Exactly.'

'So if it was Oliver who killed Daisy it's the ultimate irony. She came here because a lunatic killed the children in her school, and she herself was killed by a lunatic.'

Cordelia died six weeks later. Luke visited her every day. Sometimes they would just sit and talk, and sometimes he would read one of her favourite novels to her, by the English author Charles Dickens. When she became weaker he would carry her to the window so that she could look out at the hills.

She never once complained about her illness. If the townsfolk thought they had seen a large funeral with the deaths of Daisy and Wilbur, it was nothing compared to Cordelia's. People came from the villages around. The church doors were left open so that people outside the church could hear the service.

For weeks after the funeral Luke could be found sitting in the café in the corner seat which he and Cordelia had often occupied. Or he could be seen walking aimlessly around the hills. He had the air of a man who didn't want to be approached. The townsfolk, after expressing their condolences, on the whole left him alone.

One afternoon when Luke was sitting in his usual seat he was approached by a familiar figure. Luke glanced up. His face changed from its usual sadness to astonishment.

'Ruth! What are you doing here?'

'I thought I might have a cup of coffee.'

Luke signalled to the waitress.

'I don't understand. I thought you were still in Chicago.'

'I am. But I came to see you.'

Luke waited while the waitress brought the coffees before putting the next question.

'Is it something to do with the divorce?'

'You could say that.' She stared at him for a long time.

'If there's any money to pay, I can pay it. I've had the bounty money for killing the two outlaws. I saw to it that Stephen had his share for killing the other outlaw.'

'I know.'

'How do you know?'

'Stephen has been running an article in the *Chicago Gazette* about your exploits with the outlaws. He came to see me to fill in some of the background.'

'So you know the full story — about Cordelia's death?'

'Yes. I'm sorry. Especially about the way she died.' She stared at him as though searching for some clues in his expression.

'It's all in the past.' He stirred his coffee thoughtfully.

'Are you sure?'

'Yes. Quite sure.'

She heaved a huge sigh. 'In that case you can come home with me.'

'But — what about the divorce?'

'It hasn't gone through. I've still got the paper. When the articles about you started appearing in the newspaper and when Stephen told me about Cordelia I decided not to send them to the lawyer's.'

'So we're still married?'

'You know, sometimes you can be very quick on the uptake.' For the first time since entering the café the tension disappeared from her face. She smiled. 'So if you want to come home, you can come.'

This time it was Luke who subjected Ruth to a prolonged stare.

'Do you know — I might just do that,' he said.

THE END

VENGEANCE AT BITTERSWEET

Dale Graham

Always a loner, Largo reckoned it was the reason for his survival as a bounty hunter. But things change when he has to join forces with Colonel Sebastian Kyte in the hunt for a band of desperate killers. Kyte is not interested in financial rewards. So what is the old Confederate soldier's game? And how does a Kiowa medicine man's daughter figure in the final showdown at Bittersweet? Vengeance is sweet, but it comes with a heavy price tag.

DEVIL'S RANGE

Skeeter Dodds

Caleb Ross had agreed to join his old friend Tom Watson as a ranching partner in Ghost Creek, and arrives full of optimism. But he rides into big trouble. Tom has been gunned down by Jack Sweeney of the Rawl range, mentor in mayhem to Scott Rawl . . . Enraged, Caleb heads for the ranch seeking vengeance for Tom's murder. But, up against a crooked law force and formidable opposition, he'll have to be quick and clever if he's to survive . . .